Mouths of the Junction

I0670845

A Novel

Mohamed Gibril Sesay

Sierra Leonean Writers Series

Warima / Freetown / Accra
120 Kissy Road, Freetown, Sierra Leone
Kofi Annan Ave, North Legon, Accra, Ghana
Publisher: Prof. Osman Sankoh (Mallam O.)
publisher@sl-writers-series.org
www.sl-writers-series.org

Mouths of the Junction

Copyright © 2017 by Mohamed Gibril Sesay
All rights reserved.

ISBN: 978-9988-8698-4-7

Sierra Leonean Writers Series

To

Tha Iye

The Ladani

He was The Ladani of the land; the one who called people unto prayers. Many liked him; many didn't, especially those who loved the dregs of our palm winey sleep. Those guys would be scooping the last of the sweet dregs and this Ladani would enter the tavern of their drunken dreams with his divine alarm, "get up, up, up, oh ye mortal men and women. Before the sun rises and raises your eyes unto it, you must rise up now and raise your eyes unto the lord".

Dama said unto her husband, Orfi Usu The Policeman, "the cock of the lord has crowed; rise up".

Many people woke up, but did not get up. There were so many things to do in bed before getting up - like thinking about the many eyes that would follow your hands to see if you would dip them inside your pocket for chop money for the family; like thinking about the story to make up to convince Mamatu Cookery to give you more time to pay up; or like thinking of which clothes to wear today, since most of the clothes were worn out junk clothes picked up at the Butu and Pick Market over two years ago.

But many also did get up the soonest they heard The Ladani's call, even those who had no intention

1

of going to the mosque for prayers. There were so many things besides prayers to do in the morning. Like queuing up for water; like queuing up to bathe; like queuing up to pee.

The drunkenness of sleep could still be seen in people's gait as they queued up to pee in our special pee spaces. Some men were so drowsy that they could not hold their thing with the care necessary for a good pee, which was why the favourite first words of the morning for many a rascally man to another was, "I wish you a good pee".

"Happy peeing", said Dulai Free Talk to Santigie Ginger Da Fitter.

"Happy peeing", said Shekuna, The Poda Poda Driver to a neighbour.

"Happy peeing," said a man to another he thought was as rascally as he was. But this other man was no rascal. He took offence, and the first pee bout of the day was hatched. Blows in the dim darkness of dawn dented those they were not meant for.

Rugie The Fry-fry Seller hollered to her man, Orman The Artist, "ooo it is me, it is me, your blows are denting my back".

Orman The Artist answered, "you should not have come here, you know that even in the dark, your body attracts my hardest blows".

2

The Ladani raised his voice, "you were not called to fight; you were called unto prayers".

But over yonder, near the main junction, Madu The Mason was cussing some witches for his nightmares. "I had lots of money yesterday, today I have none; I had lots of friends yesterday, today I have none". And he hailed down bad words upon bad words upon bad words, including mammy cusses that many ears around this place loved, and the small crowd that gathered around him clapped and clapped, "you are good, you are good".

The other day Santigie Ginger Da Fitter, a man not so good at cussing attempted to cuss for being called a fool. Women shouted him down, "such uselessness, you cannot even make a good cuss". And the crowd roared with laughter at the man's rotten banana-ness. Whereupon his older friend, Dulai Free Talk, who all agreed had a mouth that had no boundaries, offered to teach the useless man how to cuss.

"Every word could be made into a good cuss," said Dulai Free Talk unto his friend. "But surprise is at the heart of the good cuss. Mix with rudeness the words that your opponent respects. Study your opponent, the good cuss is the one that takes your opponent off-balance".

A year later, the biggest cussing event in the stories of our land took place between the teacher and the student. Some judged it a draw, but many declared the student victorious on account of his commencing his cussing by first cussing his own mother a hundred and one times in about three minutes and forty-seven seconds.

Believe me when I tell you these things. I timed his cussing myself. I am not like those other story tellers who tell lies. You know, I grew up here. So believe me when I also tell you that those who know more than I also said The Ladani came to our town the year the Queen of the island once called the Sun-Never-Set Empire visited the land. The Queen came here about sixteen years after some never-before-seen bombs dropped on the people of Japan.

"That bomb was dropped during The Burma War," said The Old Man. "I fought for Churchill in Myohaung during that war. It was there that I heard that a great darkness fell from the sky; the earth shook; thousands died, the flesh of people melted; it was as if the angel Azraeel had blown the trumpet of destruction announcing the end of this world".

With the Queen's visit, some people drunk with the alcoholic maggots of some palm tree thought that the sun of The Empire had set forever here. Nonsense. Years later, that same Queen, now an old

4

lady, would give medals to persons from her kingdom who came to our land to fight some *toomboo*. They came here dressed in white plastics like masquerades from the land of the dead; they performed lots of ceremonies before they entered the areas of the fight, including spraying some strange *lasmami* and *saweh* on their shroud-like masquerades.

Some years before that *toomboo* fight, that same Queen sent her soldiers here to raid rascals that were ravishing women and cutting the throats of the people at the Hills of the Slippery Okra. The Queen's soldiers called the battle Operation Barass. It was a big-big strike against a ragtag gang of rascals commanded by a crippled General.

Ami, who everybody believed was the Wife of The Poda Poda Driver came to our community not very long after that. We also called her Ami Silencer. She was such a silent one in the community. But her silence was so attractive. No one knew much about her; no body knew her story; she was nearly story-less... So she could not be talked about in a community that liked to talk and talk. She was like some silence around which the community noise revolved. Even the talk-talk Dulai Free Talk was silent around her. Anytime he saw her, his mind ran unto something he thought he knew, but that looked hazy; "what is it o lord, what is it o lord?" he would say to himself.

Those who know more about the Ladani say he came to our town because he had 'tampered' with the youngest wife of the chief of his birthplace. His mother had told him, "run, dear son, run, run to a place where old chiefs have no power over young men being young with young women".

That was the same chief who had so feared road workers that he did not allow the new road to pass through his town. The young road workers were sugar for sugar-ant women, impregnating hundreds wherever they went, leaving behind pregnant women without husbands, and these women gave birth to children, who, with fathers unknown, were called children of the road.

That was long ago, before The Ladani gained religion in our region. He had a voice so sweet that the Imam of our town prayed, "oh lord, you know age has eaten up the voice of our old ladani; dear Lord, get that young man with that sweet voice to dedicate it to calling people to you rather than singing loose songs to revelers".

The prayers took a long time being answered. The Ladani before he became The Ladani continued to be the song-maker of the community, especially during the annual lantern competition between the different communities of the land. All remembered the song he got out the year when the seven-days rain destroyed the lantern of the community. It was the seventh day of the seven-days rain and we had hoped that it would not rain that night. But rain upon rain upon rain fell on our lantern depicting a ship berthing down the quay, complete with cranes and containers, and even thieves pushing some items down the sides, which happened to be real sweets that would fall unto the streets of the parade and real people fighting all over for them.

Great lantern, that one, the talk of the place; the rain completely destroyed it. But the song of The Ladani before he became The Ladani was not destroyed. It was sung under the heavy downpour, young men and women hugging each other, four steps forward, two steps backwards as they moved around the streets of the land:

Let's do it, ayyyy
Let's do it, I won't do it
Let's do it ayyyy
Let's do it, I won't do it
Let's do it, ayyyyy
Titi nor form o, I won't do it

"Nonsense songs," said The Old Man, "in our time, songs had meaning, but what's the meaning of this song?"

"True say talk me, so let me say the truth," said The Sage. "The song means whatever you take it to mean. If you take it to be a rude song, so be it. But I also see a song of resistance. Young men are asking young women to do funny things, but the young women are wisely saying no".

The Old Imam continued to pray for the conversion of the song-maker. It took a long time, but it finally happened. The Ladani before he became The Ladani saw a woman he wanted to marry. He came to The Old Imam to ask him to lead a band of Muslims to meet the father of the woman. "Please Imam," he said, "the father of the woman I want to marry would not allow it. When I told him I am a song-maker he grunted the grunting of a man with a toothache, mouth closed, nostrils vibrating with air from deep within his soul. And he started crying like a gluttonous child who had just been stopped from eating too much in the evening because he woke up his sleeping mother to piss a lot at night anytime he ate a lot in the evening".

"Oh no," said The Old Imam, "you don't describe a father in law that way. Your problem is your descriptions. Even in your songs, it is your

8

descriptions that make many people think of many immoral things".

"Imam, forgive me my descriptions, I truly want that woman for a wife, and if it means changing the way I describe, so be it".

"Describe then for the lord, the old ladani has lost his voice, we need a new ladani to call the people unto prayers, be our Ladani," said the Imam.

"So be it," The Ladani replied.

Sorie Measurement

So it was with this man, Sorie Measurement, a man of all colours, rainbow across the sky of our lives. Especially after he was caught in his inner room doing mammy-and-daddy business with Kadia, The *Ball-eye* of Kama Bluffer. Well, not exactly, you really never know the true stories around here. Kadia, The *Ball-eye* of Kama Bluffer said they were not doing mammy-and-daddy business. But somehow the story told by the tearful Kama Bluffer became the oft-repeated story. It was a battle of stories that day. They say Kama Bluffer cried as he told his, but Sorie Measurement laughed as he narrated his version, saying he was only taking measurements for some clothes he was sewing for Kadia, The *Ball-eye* of Kama Bluffer.

"True say talk me, so let me say the truth," said the Sage. "Tears make people believe your story more than laughter does".

So Kama Bluffer's story won the day; and the other story of Sorie Measurement and Kadia was thrown to the laughter of the community, taken lightly, taken like child's play, and child's play, like *botkidi, gehgeh, touch, ar die, akra, tintantu,* was not held seriously here.

10

Sorie Measurement? He was the chief tailor of our community, the very first to open a tailor shop here. He had the smallest waist of all in the community, and it was rumoured by friends that what he lacked behind he had in front of him. But The Old Imam said only foolish men would talk about the fronts of other men. So, since so many grown up men didn't want to be seen as foolish, that talk was censored. If talked about at all it was in hushed tones, amongst some men of the older generation. So that story never became an oft-repeated story. Rather it became like some secret of the old generation, unknown to most people of the younger generation. Like the story of Mr. Thompson, the spirit of the quay of the community. They say, another spirit, the one legged *Wanfut Jompi* stole his chains on Good Friday, the chains that he used to anchor his prized ship. The ship ran adrift and got lost, with its cargoes of rare goods. So Mr. Thompson banned work at the quay on Good Friday.

When I heard that story I said to the person I heard it from, "can you sign for that story?"

He laughed, "fool, where have you ever seen people signing their names under the stories of spirits?"

The younger generation did not know this story; they only knew Good Friday was a day of no work at the quay, and that the big people of the quay would kill cows to cool the heart and vexation of Mr. Thompson. Some foolish strangers once tried to work on Good Friday; sea-storms tormented them, and several of them drowned. They say *Wan fut Jumpi* has still not returned the chains. If you listen carefully in the still of the night in our community, you will hear the chains being dragged along by that one legged spirit. And you may also hear the whirling *Ronsho* - a great thief, that *Ronsho*, if you catch him, he will pay as ransom great sums that make you forever wealthy. They say Orbangu, the wealthiest man in our community had his wealth from *Ronsho*.

True, Sorie Measurement was the first tailor in the community, but he was not the best. The best tailor was Kama Bluffer. But he sewed only for his wives, or those he wanted to make wives. They say Kama Bluffer became a tailor because of a man-and-woman business between Sorie Measurement and Kadia, *The Ball-eye* of Kama Bluffer. The affair started slowly, with Sorie Measurement taking the measurement of Kadia slowly, and again and again, especially when he was measuring Kadia's waist and breast areas. He would linger therein, tightening the tape around the breast and asking, "do you want it this tight?" And Kadia would say "a little tighter". He did that again around the waist, "do you want it tight?" and Kadia answered, "little tighter". They say one day Kadia wore some very big skirt, and Sorie Measurement said, "I can't tightly measure your body in this big skirt". Kadia replied, "I can remove it if you want". Sorie Measurement was very surprised, but he nonetheless blurted a reply, "This is an open place, let's go to the inner room".

People in the know say Kama Bluffer was the very first person to call Sorie Measurement that name. Before that Sorie Measurement was called Sorie Tailor by those who went to school in our community, and Sorie Taila by those who did not. But since those who never attended school in our community were more numerous than those who went to school, the name Sorie Taila was the one to use if you wanted people to really know whom you were talking about. The old women said, "take this *mafalay* to Sorie Taila to stitch its torn parts for me". The old men said, "take this torn *dunglin* to Sorie Taila to fix for me". The middle age women said, "take this *docket en lappa* to Sorie Taila to fix for me". All amongst the middle age men, except The Teacher-writer said, "take this *kanabi* to Sorie Taila to hem the loosen bottoms". The Teacher-writer

13

said "take these trousers to Sorie Tailor to fix for me". But the young men said, "Sorie Taila, please fix my jeans". And the young women said, "please fix my awareness".

"What has awareness got to do with sewing?" asked a woman new to the ways of our community.

I answered, "awareness was the name of the tight fitting trousers girls and young women wore under their skirts or under their other trousers to prevent big-men big-fool from ravishing them. But these stories of ravishing were not stories talked about loudly; they were too shameful for the community. So we whispered them around, so that two-three ears wouldn't hear about them - like the story of that big man who on being caught by his wife ravishing his fourteen year old step daughter defended himself by saying, "how can I cook a soup without tasting it?" Or like that other big white *alaki* fowl who was caught putting his hand under the skirt of his neighbour's ten years old daughter. These stories were mainly whispered about, but mothers took practical steps and bought awareness for their daughters as both a reminder of and a resistance to the big-men big-fools".

So it was that even girls as young as ten would say, "Sorie Taila, please make my awareness, it got torn whilst I was playing *akra*".

14

Those were times when things were really difficult in the community and most people went to Sorie Taila to fix torn things. And this was why Dulai Free Talk called Sorie Taila Sorie Patch Patch, The Chief of Patchers. But that name did not stick. It reflected too much on so many people in the community who went to Sorie Patch Patch to patch up their torn fabrics. The community censored it; but Dulai Free Talk was not one to be censored. He kept on calling him Sorie Patch Patch much to the annoyance of the elders of the community. So it was sort of a great relief when Kama Bluffer called Sorie Taila Sorie Measurement, and Dulai Free Talk adopted it, and popularized it, embellishing the story of the name to the funniest degrees possible.

"It was about Kadia, The *Ball-eye* of Kama Bluffer," Dulai Free Talk told us. "Somebody told Kama Bluffer that Sorie Taila liked to take the measurements of beautiful women in his inner room, especially so the measurements of Kama Bluffer's very own *ball-eye*, Kadia. One day, Kama Bluffer bought some beautiful fabrics for his Kadia. Kadia took them to Sorie Taila some few houses down the road to get Sorie Taila to sew them into something very beautiful and one-in-town. Thirty Minutes passed, Kadia did not return. Thirty-five minutes; Kadia did not return. One hour; Kadia did

15

not return. One hour thirty minutes; Kadia did not return. Kama Bluffer rushed to the tailor shop, and asked, "where is Sorie Taila?" One of the apprentices, a new one, just a week into his apprenticeship and so he did not know the lies and false stories of the tailor shop shouted, "Sorie Taila is taking measurements of Kadia in his inner room". Kama Bluffer rushed towards the door, shouting, "what is this about these measurements in your inner room; why must you do our women's measurements in your inner room? Is that what your tailoring is all about? Are you Sorie Tailor or Sorie Measurement? Tell me, should we now call you Sorie Measurement?"

But even with that, Sorie Measurement remained a popular tailor, though men were now more watchful of their ball-eye women who went to him for measurements.

Satu said, "only Mamatu's Cookery Shop has more frequent customers that Sorie Measurement's Tailor Shop".

"No way," said Dama, The Wife of Orfi Usu, "Customers only go to Mamatu's Cookery Shop in the morning, people visit Sorie Measurement's Tailor Shop all the time, from sunrise till sunset".

"Most of the persons who go to Sorie Measurement's Tailor Shop are not customers; they are idlers; they just sit there all day with all sorts of stories," said the first wife of Foday Voice. "The only time that I think his shop has more real customers than Mamatu's Cookery Shop is around pray-day".

"Big story teller; last pray-day, he said he would finish my pray-day clothes before pray-day morning, but he was nowhere to be seen that morning".

"Me too, " said Dama, "my whole family had to wear old clothes to the praying field".

"You're lucky," said the first wife of Foday Voice, "you had good old clothes. I had none. I worked hard to get those materials I took to him, but he disappointed me".

Ami Silencer, who everybody believed was The Wife of The Poda Poda Driver passed by the women discussing Sorie Measurement. Silence. She smiled and continued her walk. She met Dulai Free Talk around the junction. She smiled at him. Her smiles tugged at Dulai Free Talk's heart - like some bush rope drawing bushes and the bushes drawing indistinct things.

Kama Bluffer

They say soonest after he caught Sorie Measurement taking the measurements of the almost naked Kadia, Kama Bluffer made a vow to learn to sew so that his lovers would never again go to tailors for measurements. He went to tailor shops far and near to learn his trade. From his own mouth, we learned he went to twenty-four such shops, learning all sorts of cutting, sewing, hemming, and ironing ways.

But many doubted this number, especially so Dulai Free Talk, and he called Kama Bluffer Kama Two Dozen on account of that. Kama Bluffer hated that name. No body would call him that, except when they had quarrels with him. "Kama Two Dozen, Kama Two Dozen," they would say. And Kama Bluffer would become very annoyed, and he would say things that would turn people against him when the dispute came before the elders for judgment. "Oh no Kama Bluffer," the elders would say, "you should not have said such bad-bad words against his mother because he called you that, no, no, no, no".

Ami Silencer once heard the elders admonish Kama Bluffer that even the hottest temper could not cook rice. She smiled when she heard that. Dulai Free Talk saw her smile, and his heart nearly jumped out of his heart-case. "This Ami Woman; this Ami woman," he said quiety to himself.

Kama Bluffer became the best tailor for female clothes. Women yearned his rare designs. When he wanted a woman he would sew some great clothes and send them over to her. The clothes would stop and go, stop and go, in a bait-like way to get the woman to give him an answer. Some women gave him a yes answer after a few clothes; some would hold out for more. Some women returned the clothes with mild answers of no; but we would never forget two women, great friends, who came rushing with the clothes to Kama Bluffer and rained on him such bad-bad words that Dulai Free Talk said the smelliness of those words would only be washed off Kama Bluffer with a thousand folded-fist-size balls of black soap and five thousand buckets of water.

Two women never gave Kama Bluffer an answer, and never returned the clothes. One was Ami Silencer, who everybody believed was the wife of The Poda Poda Driver. People watched to see what she would do with the clothes. Nothing. She never returned them; and there were no rumours around what she did with the clothes.

Kama Bluffer's closest friend asked him, "why would you want another man's woman?"

Kama Bluffer replied, "I don't want her; and I am on oath never to reveal the reasons for the clothes".

"But what is she doing with the clothes; we've never seen her wear them".

"I don't know," said Kama Bluffer.

"Nobody knows," said the friend. "No one can read the *samba letter* of Ami Silencer.

Not so the other woman who did not return the clothes and never gave Kama Bluffer an answer. Her *samba letter* was being read all over the place. They say that she sent these clothes to her sister overseas who sold them for huge sums with the brand name 'Bluffer'. Some said the clothes were sold in other towns in the country. There were so many stories about what that woman did with the clothes. This place was a place of many stories about the same thing.

They say Kama Bluffer would divorce wives who grew out of the clothes he sewed for them. He would say, "you have no shape; I don't want you again".

Later, when he grew older, and clung on to religion, Kama Bluffer would divorce women for a different reason - "you have no religion, you don't behave according to the dictates of the faith, I don't want you again".

20

But Dulai Free Talk sneered, "it's the same, the same; the monkey never leaves its left-handed tricks behind; bedbugs can always be found in an old mattress. The only women Kama Two Dozen sacks are those who grow out of his styles. His faith has not changed him; it has only given him another story for his actions".

But two of the women whom Kama Bluffer sacked said he sacked them because they had good opinion of Sorie Measurement. He had asked them, "what do you think of Sorie Taila?" One of the women replied, "we grew up together, he's a good man".

The other woman replied, "he's a good friend of my sister; he sews her clothes".

Kama Bluffer held that against them. One morning, because the two women did not answer to the call of The Ladani, he sacked them. "You have no religion, I don't want you again".

Foday Voice

We called him Foday Sorry Voice, though most just cut it short and called him Voice. They say he had a most sorrowful voice at the height of his begging career. He would say, "give me for God, give me for His Prophet. May God add more unto the place where this is coming from; may your enemy be put to shame, may your voice be on top of all voices wherever you are; now that you have fed a hungry man, may you always have food on your table; may your rice always have good sauce on top of it; with red-red palm oil, and beef and chicken and fish".

One day The Teacher-writer objected to his prayer, "I don't want lots of palm oil on my sauce o, please I don't want lots of palm oil on my sauce".

So Voice changed the prayer for him, "may your sauce have no palm oil, no fish and no beef".

The Teacher-writer was taken aback, "no I did not say I don't like fish and chicken and beef, only palm oil; please pray for me again". That was the first time there was an argument about his prayers.

"True say talk me,' so let me say the truth," said The Sage, "not all prayers are good, just don't accept prayers from people like that; some prayers are damn right stupid, some are very old, and of no use today, some are just not good for some regions -

would you pray for rain in a place of so much rain that floods kill people every time? Would you pray for bread where people love rice more than everything, where if they haven't eaten rice they would say they have not yet eaten even when they would have already eaten two dozen loafs of bread?"

Ami Silencer heard The Sage say this. She smiled and went into her house.

The other time Voice prayed a Muslim prayer for a Christian. "Fisabillah," Voice said, " do it for Allah and His prophet".

The Christian man replied, "say Alleluia, in Jesus name".

Voice was confused; the Christian man was wearing some big gown, like Muslims did. Muslims and Christians were increasingly wearing the same clothes. Before, you knew Muslims by their gowns, and Christians by their suits. But now Christians and Muslims all wore gowns; and all also wore suits, they looked so much the same. The beggars did not know how to distinguish between them, and this was bringing confusion to their prayers: "O Allah, give this man who gave us food what ever he desires, In Jesus' Name we pray, Inshallah". "Alleluia, do it for Jehovah and His Prophet Mohamed, may Allah Grant you janat firrdaws".

"It is religious tolerance," said The Sage, "but when truth says "say me," I have no choice but to say this truth - it is religious tolerance based on religious stupidity and mix-up".

They say Voice started begging very young, after his parents abandoned him as a bad-luck child. He was playing in one of the stony streets of our community when he fell, unable to get up. His legs shriveled.

Nurses at the clinic asked Voice's mother whether Voice was given the polio vaccine. Voice's mother said no. The nurses also asked, "did your son have high fevers in the last few days?"

Voice's mother replied, "yes, but I soaked towels in water and placed them on him and his body cooled down".

The nurses further asked, "was he complaining of muscle pain? Was he having difficulty walking in the last few days?"

Voice's mother replied, "I would not know, I usually left him in the care of my sister-in-law and neighbours when I went to sell my wares at the market. But they told me everything was alright with him, and that he was very active, playing *touch* with his mates when he suddenly fell down and could not get up".

The nurses said Voice had polio, that some nerves connecting his head, backbone and foot had some problems.

"What are nerves?" Voice's mother asked.

"These are like wires taking orders from the brain to order parts of the body. These wires may now have connection problems in some places".

"Please reconnect the wires," Voice's mother cried, "I want my child to walk again". But the legs continued to shrivel.

A woman of the community advised, "get your child out of that hospital, this is not some normal sickness for the hospital".

Voice's mother got Voice out of the clinic and took him to the medicine man. The medicine man said Voice bucked his right toe against some bewitched stone, and could not get up because of that. He said there were several such stones now in the community, put there by bad people sacrificing the 'walking' of children to an evil spirit. "The cursed stones must be found and destroyed, else Voice would never walk again, else children in the community were at risk of bucking their feet against the cursed stone and becoming paralysed, else even adults who buck their right toe on it would have bad luck and may be sacked from their offices that day, or have their wares seized, or get themselves thrown for nothing into police cells, or they may have their spouses fall into the hands of a person with loose morals".

The medicine man went into action, uprooting several stones in the community, dousing them with spiritual liquids, and smashing them with his hammer.

No effect. Voice's legs continued to shrivel.

They took Voice to the old ladani, not the one who was a song-maker, but the one before him. They say that old ladani was a master of *kalwa* whose incantations had healing powers. "Didn't you see how he healed my head ache", said the *arborbor* seller. "I had taken all sorts of medicine, but the headache persisted. One day he came to my house and heard me complain about the headache. He stood over me, read words over my head, and since that time I have not had these painful headaches".

The old ladani spat into his hands, rubbed the hands together and gently caressed Voice's head, all the while intoning Arabic words. He did this for seven days.

No effect. Voice's legs continued to shrivel.

Dulai's mother pointed Voice's mother to a new man of God who was filled with healing powers. The man of God took them over for some whole night prayer, and gave them holy water; and cried that Voice would be healed if only he believed.

"The truth says "say me," so let me say the truth, that's nonsense," said The Sage, "what has a child's faith got to do with healing?"

But the man of God continued his sermon, "if he only has faith, if only he has faith, healing is on the way".

No effect. Voice's leg continued to shrivel.

Months passed, Voice' mother got tired of taking him from one place to another. Other chores took her time - like going to the market to sell; like cooking the day's meal when she returned in the evening; like getting pregnant again, and giving birth to another child whilst doing all the other chores. Slowly, slowly, Voice was abandoned to fend for himself. His shriveled leg made him a friend of the soil; dirt was always on him.

"He's dirty", said the *ogi* maker.

"He's a bad luck child," said the *ogiri* seller.

"His feet have evil marks," said the *arborbor* mammy

"He plays with evil spirits," said the wrapper of *agidi*.

Mothers warned their kids not to play with him. But because they thought he played with evil spirits, they were also a little afraid of hurting him.

"Be careful with him, he may hurt you," the *kongu* woman warned. "If he sees you eating and asks for some, give him, else he uses your refusal to summon you unto his evil spirits and do great harm to you".

So it was that the community closed off all opportunities for contacts with the Voice except that of a beggar and benefactors. So it was that Voice homed his skills on this, with a most sorrowful voice and statements at once cajoling and threatening, at once uplifting and belittling. It started with begging for food. But as he grew older he found out that begging for money was better than begging food, for with money he could get many more things. He got better and better at begging, intoning the primary words of begging - fisabillah - like a mother would sing a dirge for a beloved infant. Voice caressed these words, holding onto the syllables liked he did not want to let them off, but that he should go to the other syllables to give meaning and relevance to all of them -fiiiiiiii saaaaaaa biiiiiiii liiiiiiillll llllllllah waaaaaaa liiiiii raaaaaaa suuuuuul liiiiiiiillll llllllahhhhh. People flocked to give him money, sometimes forming long queues. He was everybody's favourite beggar. And he earned more money than what he needed for food.

He grew into a fine young man with great arms but weak legs; and he acquired the desires of young men - not clothes, for being so close to the floor in the dusty streets of the community, his clothes got dirty too quick, obscuring whatever good quality they had. Not music, for how would he enjoy anybody's song when from sunrise until sundown he was singing his own sorrows in the soils of the land watching the soles of people? So he knew that what he desired were neither fancy clothes nor music. He did not have a name for what he desired, but he sure knew that these desires were triggered by skirts of women brushing against his face as he sat in the mud of his begging.

One day Madu The Mason asked him, "Voice, do you want a woman?"

"No," he replied, "which woman would want a man like me".

"They would, you never know, give me some money, let me go see what I can do".

Voice gave Madu The Mason some money. Two days passed; Madu The Mason came again, "the money you gave me was not enough; give me more".

Voice gave him more.

A week later, he came again. "We are almost there," he said, "just a little more, and I'll bring her for you".

Voice gave him more.

Five days later, he came again. "The woman is ready for you, but where will you take her? She said she would not visit you in the veranda where you sleep. We need to find a room".

Voice gave him money for a room.

Eight days later, he came again. "I have secured a room; I need money for a bed".

Voice asked, "can I go see the room?"

Madu The Mason said, "Oh we need to put the bed therein before I show it to you. It is a beautiful room, on the side of the house, away from the noisy entrance on the other side. Nobody will see who goes there. Look at the keys, take them; I'll hold onto the spare, because I need to put the bed there. Let me have the money for the bed".

Voice took the keys and gave him money for the bed.

Four days later he came again, "I have fixed the bed. Beautiful bed, very strong. But I need money to buy bed sheets".

Voice replied, "I know where good bed sheets are sold, I'll go buy them".

"No, no, no, you don't," Madu The Mason said.

"Yes, yes, yes, I do," Voice shouted.

"Oh no, no, no, don't shout," said Madu The Mason, "this is between you and I".

"I'll shout, I'll shout, it is my money, I'll shout". And with that Voice jumped at him, clasping the open ends of the collar of Madu The Mason's shirt.

Crowds gathered, and that was how the community knew that Voice had desires for women, and that he would do whatever it took to have them.

So it was that Voice started to have women; so it was that he decided to marry one of them. She was a young woman, very beautiful. She turned down many able bodied men for Voice. News spread that Voice might have bewitched her with his evil powers. The parents of the woman refused to accept Voice's kola. But the Woman was determined. She and Voice rented a room and moved in. She was the first *taptomi* in our community, the first woman who moved in with a man without being married. Months later she gave birth to a son. The community held its collective breath, waiting to see if the curse of the woman's father that her children would turn up crippled could come to pass. The woman got pregnant again, and again, and again. She vaccinated all of the children; none got shriveled legs.

Voice did mammy-and-daddy business with several other women. They say he once had a one-night stand with a tipsy man-starved high-class woman who had asked a friend to get her a strong man. The friend got Voice and in the dark of a blackout night brought him to the room of the tipsy woman's room. Voice worked hard that night. Early morning, when light returned, the man-starved woman, now sober, saw the crippled beggar on her bed, "what! you?" she hollered.

"Yes, me," Voice replied, waving his shriveled legs at her, "you shout it out now, it has happened; you don't shout out, it has happened. So it's better not to shout it out, for you will be the one that would be more ashamed".

The woman forever kept her peace; though whenever she saw Voice, she remembered him waving his shriveled legs and saying, "you shout it out, it has happened; you don't shout it out it has happened".

"The truth says 'say me', so let me say the truth," said The Sage, "these things happen. People did man-and-woman business in their youth that would now get them to say, "what was I feeling? What was I thinking? Look at how that person has turned out to be, look at how that person has become so foolish, look at how that person has become a drunk, look at how that person has become a thief, look at how that person has become so very nasty". And what a painful pain if those persons would want to boost their standing by telling the story of their intimate friendship with you, "see that pastor, he was always in my room". "See that Haja, we used to run things". "See that councilor, she had an abortion for me". "See that stern looking no nonsense businessman, he was so in love with me that he cried like a starving beggar for forty days and forty nights when I left him".

Some of the women Voice had man-and-woman-business with got pregnant. He ended up marrying two of these. And his three wives altogether got him thirteen children - ten girls and three boys. But people say he also had many 'point-finger children'- children that one would only point at discreetly as one's own, for the mothers had given them to other men, and you dared not claim them as your own. But only a small number of people in the older generation know about these things; and they kept these stories away from the younger generation.

Like what I heard was the reason for all the elders not agreeing to a marriage between Kama Bluffer and Satu. Kama Bluffer's father was so very kind to Satu and her mother; he always said such kind words about Satu, "waw, she's growing so fine, so well trained, so very beautiful". So Kama Bluffer had always seen Satu in a very good light. They fell in love after Kama Bluffer became the best tailor in the community and he started sewing great clothes for her. Kama Bluffer told his father, "Father, I want to marry Satu". His father replied, "over my dead body". Kama Bluffer went to his uncle, the one he hid nothing from, "Uncle O, please talk to father for me; he has refused to give his permission for me to marry Satu". His uncle replied, "over my dead body". Kama Bluffer went to his father's best friends, the ones they would always be seen playing draught and Ludo together at the other junction of the community that youths avoid. The friends replied, all of them at once, "over our dead bodies". Kama Bluffer cried, "why is every one saying "over my dead body, over my dead body". An aunt called him aside, "listen Kama Bluffer, your father liked woman-business a lot in his youth. Satu is his daughter. Your father was afraid of going forward and claiming responsibility because Satu's mother was married. No my dear, you cannot marry Satu, she's your sister".

Voice worked very hard at begging to take care of his large family. But bad-hearted people started bad-mouthing him, announcing that he was richer than the people he begged from. He started going very far to beg, away from where they knew him. This took a huge toll on him. Especially so when he had always refused a wheel chair, saying that being on the ground, dragging one's waist in the mud brought in greater sorrowing from givers. And made givers feel superior, and they would give him more money because they felt good doing that.

And then he met more aggressive beggars, and these were mostly on wheelchairs. They moved very fast, chasing slow moving cars in the traffics of the rushed hours of the morning and evening. Voice's earnings dropped; he could not face the competition from these new beggars, who would loudly bless to entice givers and sometimes loudly cuss those who would not give them. "God will hammer you," they said.

"Why would beggars cuss?" a stranger to the ways of our communities once asked Orbangu, The Businessman.

"My own cousin cursed me more than that," Orbangu replied. "My cousin said it was the luck of the family that was gathered unto making me; that if I did not share with them they would take back the family luck and blessing and leave me so destitute that I would compete with dogs for food at the community dirt dump".

Voice most times now returned home empty handed. Two of his wives, the younger ones and eight of his children abandoned him, not wanting to be associated with a failed beggar.

Dulai Free Talk said, "mortal man is like the weather that changes and changes". Ami Silencer heard him say this. She smiled at him. Dulai Free Talk smiled back; Ami Silencer was the only person before whom Dulai Free Talk seemed lost for words. Some special things about her locked his words. He felt connected to her; not any ordinary connection, but some deep-deep connection.

Foday Voice also heard Dulai Free Talk say "mortal man is like the weather". He replied, "it is true my brother, look at me, my own blood running way from me".

Foday Voice retired from street begging, and would spend hours on end brooding about times past when beggars were milder, when people were not like the weather; when relatives were kinder and his voice was stronger.

He was brooding thus one evening when an urchin led unto him a very beautiful young woman with two police officers as guards. "Are you Pa Foday Sorry Voice?" The Beautiful Young Woman said in some accent very different from the way people in the community spoke.

Fear caught Voice, for this was a place where visits by such distinguished persons spelt trouble; especially so when they came with police officers. The young urchin who led them unto Voice was dragged away by his mother, "you want to give people trouble; you want to give people trouble?"

"No," said The Beautiful Young Woman, "I am not here to give anybody trouble. My mother said I must come to this place to look for Pa Foday Voice".

"Peace be unto you; who is your mother?" asked The Old Imam who had been called to soften the situation in case it spelt trouble for someone in the community.

The Beautiful Young Woman told them.

"Oh yes, yes I remember her," said The Old Woman, who was part of a delegation of old people called to serve as frontline to diffuse any trouble. The old woman continued, "Your mother was the wife of Orbangu who owned five trailers that were transporting goods from the ports. Orbangu did not go to school; he married your mother because he wanted a very close book-woman who could do all the paperwork. Her father stopped her schooling so that she could be married to Orbangu. She left this place with her little daughter when Orbangu died, taking everything with her. So you are her daughter, where is she?"

"She is dead," said The Beautiful Young Woman.

The older women started crying, "oh God, she was a good woman; she would give us money to

37

start our businesses; she would give us chop money when our husbands failed to, and our businesses did not make enough to enable us to cook for the day; she helped us pay the debts we were unable to pay. Oh God bless her, may God give her heaven for nothing; may God take away the heavy part from you, our daughter, may God make it light for you".

"Are you Pa Foday Voice?" The Beautiful Young Woman asked Voice again.

The fear gone now, Voice answered, "yes'.

There and then, The Beautiful Young Woman hugged him, sobbing, "you are my father; mother said you are my father; those were the last words she said to me, that I should come to this place and look for you".

The Beautiful Young Woman took Voice to her home in the fine outskirts of the communities of our land. She gave money and helped meet the thousand and one problems of the siblings and stepmother who stayed with Voice after his earnings from begging dropped. The other women and siblings came rushing back. Voice turned his back on them. They went to The Ladani to lead a begging mission for them to Voice. Voice accepted them back.

But Voice still missed his begging days. He continued to brood over it in the veranda of The

Beautiful Young Woman's house on the hills overlooking the communities of the land. When The Beautiful Young Woman asked him, he said, "I miss my begging days, I miss my songs, I miss the feel of satisfaction on people as they gave unto me sitting on the floor".

"True say talk me,' so let me say the truth," said The Sage, "the ways of poverty are difficult to leave behind. Even where you may now have the means, habits formed by poverty would stay with you for quite some time".

"Please, let me return to the streets," Voice asked The Beautiful Young Woman. His wives tried to dissuade him from it; they couldn't; he still brooded. His daughters tried to dissuade him from it; they couldn't; he still brooded. His sons tried to dissuade him from it; they couldn't; he still brooded. They called The Ladani to beg him out of it; he couldn't; he still brooded.

They called The Old Imam. The Old Imam said unto him, "it is in the Holy Book, 'when thou hast receiveth the bounties of your lord, announce it.' Let your new found bounties show on you, that's the way to announce unto the world the favours you have received from the lord".

Voice did not heed The Old Imam's homily. He still brooded.

So The Beautiful Young Woman struck a deal with him. He would beg for two days every week, Thursdays in the streets and Fridays at the mosque. Voice beamed with joy as he sang the beggar's refrain - *fisabilillah, fisabillah wali rasulillah.*

And he brought home lots of money, which he gladly showed unto his wives and children. The Beautiful Young Woman smiled, for unknowingly to all of them, she had employed several persons as benefactors, and she gave them lots of money to give unto Voice every Thursday and Friday as he sang in the muds of his begging.

Madu The Mason

The foundation of the house where The Ladani was residing was travelling towards the gutters, and The Ladani called Madu The Mason to stop it.

The Ladani asked Madu The Mason, "how much do you want me to pay you to fix the foundation?"

Madu The Mason replied, "we are neighbours, pay whatever you want".

The Ladani did not like this, "no tell me, you should know how much your skill is worth".

The Teacher-writer was incensed, "why do our people always want to outsource the determination of their worth to others? He who determines your worth controls you. State your worth man, state your worth".

I shook my head approvingly. It was as if Madu The Mason saw me, for he said "okay," and stated the worth of his work.

The Ladani agreed to pay Madu The Mason what Madu The Mason asked him to. He then asked Madu The Mason for the materials he would need

Madu The Mason gave a list to him.

The Teacher-writer looked at the list and laughed, "why is it that one finds the greatest number of misspelt words in our country in the lists of masons, auto mechanics and carpenters?"

Ami Silencer, who everybody thought was The Wife of The Poda Poda Driver passed by; she looked at the men; she smiled and went her way. An interlude of embarrassing silence ensued. The Ladani broke the back of the embarrassment by telling Madu The Mason he had a friend he would go buy the materials from.

Madu The Mason said, "well, in that case you would have to pay me more".

The Ladani was confused, "but we have already agreed on what I should give you for this work".

"That was then, before I knew that you, and not I, would go buy the materials. So you would have to pay me more".

"What, so you would have gotten some money from buying the materials?"

This angered Madu The Mason, "so you think I want to steal your money?"

"No, I did not say that. Okay, no problem; I will give you the money to go buy the materials".

"I would need some advance, I need to rent a shovel and a trowel, and even a rubbing board".

The Teacher-writer said, "what, those things are basic tools, every mason worth his salt should have them".

"Shut up, shut up," Madu The Mason shouted. "Who made you a commentator over our match?

Why don't you go to the stadium to run commentaries on football matches? If you don't stop rubbing your mouth on my business, journalists will sell the story of what I would do unto you".

The Ladani said, "I would like you to start the work tomorrow, here is the advance and the money for the materials".

"No problem, first thing in the morning, I will be here. No, not exactly the first thing. Coming here will be the second thing. The first thing I will do is go to Mamatu's Cookery Shop; man must eat before working".

Ami Silencer, who everybody believed was The Wife of The Poda Poda Driver heard Madu the Mason make the promise. She smiled and went her way. But she nearly bumped into Dulai Free Talk coming from the opposite direction. Dulai Free Talk smiled, and in his heart said, "there is something about this woman that I feel connected to, but I just can say".

The next morning, The Ladani waited for Madu The Mason. No show. He asked his neighbour, Dama, the wife of Orfi Usu. She replied, "I saw the foolish man at Mamatu Cookery's Shop a moment ago buying food for himself and ten of his friends".

The second morning, The Ladani again waited for Mason. No show. He asked Dama again, "did you see Madu The Mason for me?"

Dama replied, "we just quarreled moments ago at Mamatu's Cookery Shop. He was trying to shove me off the queue. But you know me, I stood my ground".

The third morning, the Ladani again waited for Madu The Mason. No show. He again asked Dama, "did you by any chance see Madu The Mason for me this morning?"

Dama replied, "he is always at Mamatu's Cookery Shop in the morning, why don't you go meet him there?"

"No, no, no," the Ladani shouted, "that place is bewitched; that woman plays with something".

Some days later, The Ladani caught up with Madu The Mason. Madu The Mason said, "Ladani, I have a funeral. The woman with whom my mother used to pound cassava leaves died, and mother asked me to represent her at the funeral. You know our mothers, they would come pestering you to attend one occasion after another. I will go do the work after the funeral".

Weeks passed, Madu The Mason did not show up. When the Ladani caught up with him again, he said, "believe you me, Ladani, I have another funeral. My former landlord lost his wife. She died bleeding after giving birth; they said there was no blood to give her. The baby survived. So sad; that woman was very good to me when I was in their house. They took her corpse to her home-village for burial. These people, they said they would not bury her here amongst total strangers; they did not want total strangers to be her grave's neighbours. And they did not like the fact of people stepping all over graves here during funerals, or sitting on the graves saying idle things. So they took her corpse to their village. They got us to spend lots of money on transport to go there. I even used part of the advance you gave me to *put kasankay* and pay my transport fares. But I will be at your place next tomorrow. Tomorrow is the naming ceremony of the child she died giving birth to. I should not miss that, she was such a good woman".

He did come the day after the naming ceremony, and cleared dirt away from the place on the foundation that he should work on. He told the Ladani he was going to bring some materials. He did not show up again that day.

When The Ladani caught up with him, he said, "look Ladani, the soonest I left your place that morning, I met my cousin's wife vomiting all over the place. You know my cousin travelled; so I had to take the woman to the hospital. I think she is pregnant. That my cousin; his wife is always on one pregnancy after another. She has given birth to eight children already. My cousin said since I did not have many children, his wife was giving birth to children for me. Interesting man, my cousin. But Ladani, I swear by all my children, I will be at your place next tomorrow morning".

Madu The Mason did not spoil his promise. He was there second thing in the morning, and started digging where he would need to pour concrete on before putting the foundation blocks. He also brought in some stones, and told The Ladani that he was going for more stones. It was around noon; he did not return to the worksite that day.

Madu The Mason returned a week later with some piles of stones, some sand and six half-bags of cement. "Ladani," he said, "you won't believe this, when I went later that day to buy the stones, the prices had changed. I told myself to wait until the next day, may be the sellers would be broke and would reduce their price. No way. I waited for another day, no way. The third day, no way. The price was a little right yesterday, so I bought the stones, and got the cement later in the day".

They say Madu The Mason lots of time bought stolen cement from a shop opened right across from a building site. That shop closed after the building was completed, prompting many stories about the shop and its owner. "He got the materials of his shop from the materials stolen at the building site," said Orman. "Yes o," said Santigie Ginger Da Fitter, "and even the owner of that site would buy nails and other little things from that shop when there were some urgent need for these things and the owner couldn't get to town to buy them". And a third man added to the story, "man live by man". And a fourth man said, "a classic case of a man using the person's own oil to fry him. I heard the shop owner sold the materials almost twice the normal price to the man". Dulai Free Talk asked him, "how do you know that?" The man replied, "don't you know, the wife of the owner of the site is the cousin of the schoolmate of my landlord's former wife. So don't argue with me when I say I know about these people". Dulai Free Talk replied, "hmmm, the way you give evidence is crazier than the run of a fowl let loose just after its head had been cut off".

Madu The Mason cleared a spot near the trench he had dug, put some sand on the cleared spot, mixed the sand with cement, put some half-inch stones, poured water and mixed sand, cement and half-inch stones into a concrete and poured the concrete on the trench.

But the concrete was not enough; it only filled about three feet of the seven feet of the trench. He asked The Ladani, "you would have to give me more money; the money you gave me for materials is finished".

The Ladani thought about hiring another mason. Afterwards this was not a small town or village where there was only one mason or carpenter and one needed to be nice to him to get him not to say, "wait until after the harvest;" or "wait until the next rainy season;" or "I won't do it because you hissed at me". But he had already started paying this mason; his money was already on him, he must not let him go. He asked him, "how much?"

Madu The Mason told him; it was almost as high as the money The Ladani had first given him, "things are going up," he said, "things are going up".

The Ladani said, "I will give you half of that".

"No problem," replied Madu The Mason, "this is only because of you; you are like family to me, a person you have known for so long is like family to you"

Momoh The Corpse Washer

He was a big-high man, Momoh The Corpse Washer, like *Gambay horse*. But an old woman who knew his babyhood told me that there were no signs of that bigness at his birth. He was thinner than fence-stick. Infact, he was born thinner than all the babies born into our community that year. And for a few months he held that record, until there was born unto us a girl whom many thought was thinner than him. The constant comparison as to who was thinner led to bets in our community that were settled by letting the girl and the boy stand next to each other.

This standing by each other almost everyday got the boy and the girl to become inseparable friends. So much so that at a tender age community people started calling them husband and wife. So much so that the boy and the girl started seeing themselves as husband and wife. So much so that their families would approve of them being husband and wife when they came of age.

The girl was never comfortable as a person on whom bets were placed. But she could not resist the tips she was given by the gamblers. One day she asked an older cousin, "what do I do to be fatter?"

The cousin replied, "eat more!"

The girl replied, "but I don't like the food prepared at home".

"Be part of the food preparation, be so active that the chores of cooking could not be done without you; be so relevant to the cooking that you become the person who is trusted to cook. Then you will cook the food the way you like it. And once you like it, you will eat more. And once you start eating more, you will grow fat. And once you start growing fat, you will grow fatter, and then you will be the fattest".

The girl did as she was told, and by age thirteen, she had become the one trusted to do the cooking. And she cooked in ways that were pleasing to her mouth. And she called her thin boyfriend to join her; and the twain started loving to eat. And they ate and ate and ate, not only what the girl cooked, but also roast-roast, fry-fry other *cham-cham*. And they grew fat, fatter, fattest. The bets shifted from who was thinnest to who could eat more.

One such competition nearly killed the boy. His belly was so full from eating two dozen loafs of bread and a bucket of pap that the food pushed for space up his gullet, blocking the passageways of air unto his lungs. His breathing slowed down. But his urge to finish eating the meal set before him was stronger than his urge to breathe. He continued eating. The girl, seeing death in his eyes, stopped eating and kicked the food from under his feet. Seven strong men held the big-eating boy tight, and the big-eating girl, bigger now than ever before, lay down on the big-eating boy's belly. She went up and down, like one doing press-up, but moving diagonally up as the full weight of her big body hit the belly of the fat boy, forcing the contents in his stomach to move upwards toward his mouth. Soon the contents gushed out of his mouth, freeing his gullet, and he announced his salvation by a belch that all agreed was the foulest since the founding of the community. The girl announced, "no more public eating competition between us; enough is enough."

The fence-stick thin baby turned big-eating boy became The Corpse Washer when an elderly corpse washer called him to help hold the corpse of a fat man he was washing for burial. The big-eating boy, now in his late teens showed no fear. Rather he loved it, and he started helping the elderly corpse washer all the time, until he became an expert himself. When the elderly corpse washer was on his deathbed, he requested from his student, "please let no other person see my nakedness when I die. You alone must wash my body".

They say the old corpse washer called Ami Silencer to bear witness unto this. She shook her head, smiled and went her way.

"That may not be true," said The Sage. "Maybe it's just because of people's desire to create stories for the silent woman; it is tormenting for people to live without having stories about people living with them".

"I agree," said Dulai Freetalk, "but something about Ami Silencer connects with me, I feel it but I don't know it yet".

The younger corpse washer did as the elderly corpse washer instructed him, and never again looked back from being the only person who washed corpses given to him. People liked this - especially the old. They did not like too many people watching their shriveled nakedness. On their deathbed, tens of them asked the young big-eating Corpse Washer to be their corpse washer.

He never thought of making money out of washing corpses. He washed corpses because he loved it. But money and gifts started flowing, from grateful survivors and on some occasion on the instructions of the dead before they died.

He soon came to realise that he got more money from relatives of the dead who wanted him to keep the secrets of those respected kith and kins who died in undignified ways; or whose bodies were grotesque in ways seen as shameful in these parts. The Old Imam said those who died with faeces all over them had their lives yanked from them through the anus by the angel of death. Those who died vomiting had theirs yanked through the mouth. Those who died with their eyes open would have been staring at the horrors of a hell awaiting them.

Not that relatives and friends of the newly dead told Momoh The Corpse Washer to keep the secrets; not that, even without the money, he would divulge the nature of their deaths; not that he ever thought of telling the secrets of their body parts. His teacher had told him that the professionalism of the corpse washer was dependent on him keeping the secrets of the dead. So he had kept the secrets.

But one day, the widow of a man with split bollocks, like that of a sheep, gave him huge sums. Another time, the woman of a man with faeces all over his dead body gave him huger sums. The other day, when a never-married socialite who lived with fine clothes always covering some bad-bad sore on his shin died, a friend of the dead man gave Momoh The Corpse Washer hugest sums. "Please don't tell people about the sores; please don't. My friend had been suffering with diabetes, but you know how superstitious many people are in this place. They would say my friend was some witch-apprentice using the big sore as some drum to beat to call people onto the evil dance of evil ones in the midnights of our community".

It was at that moment that it dawned on The Corpse Washer that the greater the amount of money given unto him, the greater the desire of survivors for the secrets of their loved ones to be buried with them.

But he could not hide anything from his wife, Mamamtu Cookery. Telling each other every evening what each daily witnessed was the staple of their lives, the crown of their day. They looked forward to the recounting of their daily encounters so much so that even in the midst of those daily encounters they would be thinking about ways to recount the stories. Like those camera people of today, who spent so much time recording events that their equipment and postures got into the way of the other people participating in the event, sometimes blocking their views, sometimes not letting them see what was being done for long periods of time; sometimes not even letting the participants hear what was being said.

"So what happened today?" Mamatu Cookery asked her husband.

"I never knew the dead man had a big navel. His wife, Asi told me that he was always using some big bandage to tie tight his big navel, so that no one would see his big *doedoe*. And that he was always complaining of stomach ache. And that she told him severally that it was his squeezed *doedoe* that was rebelling, but he would not listen. And that even as sick as he was, he would insist on her bandaging his *doedoe* so that visitors could not see it. And that her husband hated his *doedoe*. And that he was so ashamed of it. And that she, Asi hated the daily ritual of bandaging his *doedoe* for him. And that was why she, Asi was asking me, as her husband's corpse washer, not to tie his husband *doedoe*; because an image of her husband buried with a band wound round his midriff would stay with her forever".

Momoh The Corpse Washer said he untied the bandage, and dressed up the body. But the dead man's navel shot up, strong, like some medium size cucumber. He tried all he could to put it down, but it would not go down. The bulge pushed the dead man's shroud upwards, forming a little hill that could be visible to all. People with rude imagination would think it was his manhood shooting up from under the shroud. So Asi, the wife of the dead man said to him, "I will not allow this; cut the navel and place it where it will not bulge".

55

"I'm very sad for Asi," said Mamatu Cookery. "Look at what she went through. Her mother-in-law was responsible for the *doedoe*. She was not bandaging Asi's husband's navel well after it was cut off at birth, so breeze entered it, and got it swollen. A few bandaging in time by the mother would have saved the wife all those years upon years of bandaging. But perhaps the father was not buying the bandages. When parents don't do things for their sons, wives tote the burden".

Many times Momoh The Corpse Washer would tell what he overheard relatives discussing in hushed tones as he moved to wash the corpse. The other day he told his wife: "Oh I heard the wife of the dead man say "I know he gasped a lot during mammy-and-daddy business, so I took it easy on him. But that new girlfriend of his, that little girl his daughter's age, must have been very rough with him, and would not stop when the man was gasping. He died on her; my husband died on her". "We know," said a brother of the dead man. "But please don't sing that in your wailing; it is too disgraceful; please".

"Those dirges you hear relatives wail during funerals," said Momoh The Corpse Washer, "they are very censored ones; they cover up lots of things".

"Only fools would wail the foolishness of their family in a gathering of people," said Mamatu Cookery.

Mamatu Cookery

Parents named their children, but Mamatu's name was given to her by her daughter. The daughter, learning to talk, could not pronounce her mother's real name - Mariatu; she said Mamatu, and the name stuck.

I did not know how everyone started calling her Mamatu, but Dulai Free Talk said, "Ah I know. Anytime her daughter called her that, Mamatu would smile, laughter so big that her molars showed; and she would give her daughter whatever she asked, especially in the morning, when she would give her more rice than the little girl could possibly eat. Her husband, Momoh The Corpse Washer also started calling her Mamatu to get her to put more rice unto his plate. Madu The Mason also said, "Mamatu please add some more unto my plate". The Teacher-writer also said, "Mamatu, please add more unto my plate". Rugie Fry-fry also said, "Mamatu please add more unto my plate". That was how the name spread, people wanted more to be added unto the food Mamatu sold every morning at her cookery shop".

Long queues formed every morning at the cookery shop of Mamatu Cookery. These were queues of hungry men, and hungry men in the community lost patience easily, especially when they saw women standing in the queue in front of them. One morning, Sorie Measurement said to Dama, the wife of Orfi Usu the Policeman who was standing before him in the queue, "shameless woman, can't you cook your own food, must you come here to torment men for the food of a woman like you?"

Dama replied, "nonsense man, why didn't you give chop-money to your wife. Look at you, you are always here, you think we don't know, that you hide from your children to come here to eat".

"It is alright for a man to eat cookery," said Sorie Measurement, "but it is so very shameful for a woman to eat cookery".

"I will eat cookery," Dama replied, "what I do with my money is none of your business".

The queue had stopped moving; plates were being collected from those who had finished eating so that they could be washed and given to those in the queue. The young girl who was collecting the plates was waiting for a man to scoop the last spoonful of rice off his plate. The man was taking his time to do this. Another man in the queue shouted at him, "hurry up man, this is not your dinning room; hand over the plate to the girl".

The man with the last spoonful of rice on his plate put his spoon down, and started singing a mishmash of Bob Marley's songs, changing words here and there, "we bellyful but den hungry; we bellyful but den hungry; who da cap fit, let them wear it".

The man in the queue shouted a curse, "God will pay you for this. We are hungry, and you are making fun of us, God will pay you for this".

The man with the last spoonful of rice on his plate replied, "when God pays me, I will buy you fine clothes so that you won't have to wear those tattered trousers; I will buy you a bag of rice every month and give you *plasas* money so you won't have to come fight with us here for the rice and *plasas* of Mamatu Cookery".

Mamatu Cookery was sitting beside a big pot of rice that was still on the fireside, though without much fire now, only enough fire to prevent the rice from going cold. Mamatu Cookery was sweating all over her body; she had a little towel around her neck to prevent the sweat from dropping unto the pot of rice from which she was scooping rice with different sizes of rubber bowls.

"Put some little more, Mamatu Cookery," said a man, "it's not stones I'm using to buy your rice".

Mamatu Cookery emptied the bowl of rice she had scooped for the man and re-scooped, but the re-scooped rice was hardly more than the first, though the man thought he saw more.

Mamatu Cookery scooped some *plasas* from the *plasas* pot and added it unto the plate of the man. "Please put some more palm-oil," the man pleaded, "palm oil gives blood, I need more blood".

Mamatu Cookery added more palm oil unto the man's plate. Not much palm oil remained on the *plasas* in the pot. So Mamatu Cookery added unto it some palm oil she had originally skimmed from the sauce unto a medium sized bowl on the floor.

Ami Silencer came to the cookery shop, with her own bowls – a rice-pan for the rice and soup-pan for the *plasas*. Her eyes met Dulai Free Talk's eyes. Silence. Dulai Free Talk said in his heart, "something about this Ami tugs me unto something that I can still not figure. I feel like I have connection with her". More silence, like some spirit is passing by. Everyone made way for the silent beauty, as she smiled, gave her bowls, paid for the food and went away.

Another man with a half finished plate of rice said, "Mamatu Cookery, add some more sauce for me, and two more *kanda*.

Mamatu Cookery did that.

The man said, "Mamatu Cookery, the *kanda* is small".

Mamatu Cookery replied, "you always grumble about the size of *kanda* here. *Kanda* is very expensive now; they come with it all the way from Guinea. Before now, *kanda* from Guinea was cheap. But they say they have started eating *kanda* there now, so the prices are going up".

A man said, "they say they used to laugh at us, saying *kanda* is for making shoes, not for eating, but our people took *kanda* eating habits there".

Another man said, "if you see where they offload those *kanda*, you wont want to eat *kanda* again, so smelly, on the dirty floor of the market. So strong, like stone".

Dulai Free Talk joined in, "my friend eat, if you know the story of so many things we are now comfortable with, you wont want anything to do with them. One day I was saying to a friend that I won't want a woman who has had many affairs. The friend said, "fool, our people say if you look at the places water pass through before they come to you, you wont drink. Look at those village streams passing through many upstream villages. Even look at these pipes bringing water to some homes here, all the way from Guma, some pipes pass through gutters, garbage bins, some got pissed upon, and more and more. My friend, too much attention to stories of where things come from would turn your heart against most of them". Look man, eat your *kanda*, it has been cleaned and boiled over and over again to soften it".

The girl who was collecting plates was paying more attention to this *kanda* talk than to collecting plates.

"What type of girl is this?" Mamatu Cookery hollered, "rather than do your work you are paying attention to adult talk. Nonsense, I will make your *kanda* suffer if you don't hurry up".

The young girl who was collecting plates to be washed moved unto some other eaters who had finished eating and took their plates to an older girl who was washing the plates. Attention moved to this older girl. "Be quick, be quick," said the cookery eaters.

But the older girl said, "I must change the water, see the water is very dirty now". She used two buckets for cleaning the plates. The first bucket was for washing the plates and the second bucket for rinsing the plates that had been washed. The water in the first bucket was very dirty now; she threw away the water from this first bucket unto the gutter. She then poured unto this first bucket the less dirty water from the second bucket. She gave the younger girl this rinsing bucket to go get water.

"Hurry up, hurry up", said the man in the queue who had been quarrelling with the man with last spoonful of rice on plate.

Every day people quarrel to get Mamatu Cookery's food; many days people fought to get a taste of her rice and *plasas* or rice and soup. "It's not for nothing," said The Ladani, "that woman has something she plays with. That's why I don't eat her cookery, she has something she plays with".

A rival of Mamatu Cookery took up this line of attack against Mamatu Cookery. He paid a group of rascals to spread the word, "Mamatu Cookery is an evil woman; she puts charms into her soup; she's a member of the underworld".

"I even heard," said one of the rascals, "that her husband helps her. He comes home with bottles of water he had used to wash corpses for his wife to put in her soups".

"Nonsense," said Dulai Free Talk. "Can't someone be good at something here without being accused of doing some hidden evil things? That's how they used to attack the Mother of Santigie Ginger Da Fitter; that there was no way Momoh Ginger would have such a beautiful wife but for his mother turning heart of The Young And Beautiful Woman upside down with some bad charms. On hearing this, The Young and Beautiful Woman said, "well, well, I loved the way the charms made me feel, I felt good, Oh God give me another man who will put the same type of evil charm that made me so happy and upside down with my husband"".

Dulai Free Talk continued, "nonsense people. That's the same they are doing with Mamatu Cookery. All I know is that Mamatu Cookery knows how to play with her hands when she cooks, and that's what makes her a good cook with the sauciest food around".

"You don't know these things," said The Ladani, "but they do exist".

But even the faith of Dulai Free Talk was shaken when months later they found entrails and teeth of a dog mixed up with the entrails of fishes in Mamatu Cookery's garbage bin. "What? Dogs? We have been eating dogs all this while?" Dulai Free Talk asked.

"What do you have to say now?" The Ladani asked Dulai Free Talk. "God, God, this woman is making us eat dog meat, oh God oh God".

The Ladani's exasperations woke up the fun side of Dulai Free Talk and he said, "well, if her cooking is so great, then the dog meat is a great ingredient, don't you think so Ladani? Let's go hunt dogs for their meat".

Later it was found out that a rascal put the dog entrails in Mamatu Cookery's garbage bin; but the damaged had been done. Many people now thought of dog meat when they ate at Mamatu Cookery's place.

Councilor Man Plus

We called her Man Plus; that was how she called herself on the night she won elections as the very first woman to be a councilor from our community. People did not take her seriously when she announced that she was contesting elections to become a councilor.

"What," said Madu The Mason, "have you ever seen a hen crowing? This woman is arrogant, she wants to be our leader".

"True say talk me, so let me say the truth. Is there a non-arrogant politician?" asked The Sage. "They say we were created equal, but there comes this man saying, let me lead you. Is there anyway you would not call this arrogance? Beloved, only say that this politician is less arrogant than that one, but all of them are arrogant".

The incumbent councilor dismissed Man Plus, "she's a stupid woman, don't mind her".

Ami Silencer was passing by when the incumbent was saying that. She smiled and went her way. Dulai Free Talk walked behind, watching her move. He said to himself, "from the way she walks, the shape of a woman I had connection with is emerging. But who? Where? Where? When? When?"

Man Plus decided to do something to get every one to take her seriously. She called twenty ladies from her Osusu group, and got them to wear the same clothes, and let each of them stand, one woman to a junction, on all the twenty junctions of our community, each woman holding on high a photograph of Man Plus.

"What audacity!" some men shouted. "loose women all over our junctions with the photos of a loose woman".

Some men went to Man Plus' husband, "what is it that we are hearing about your wife? Do you want her to be a public wife?"

"What do you mean?" the husband asked.

"Politicians are randy people; there's something in that game that makes them randy. Have you not heard that a serious politician should be serious about man-and-woman business. Your wife will join that club. And her name will be smellier than the men; for remember when men are randy, we praise them; when women are randy, we cuss them".

The husband called Man Plus and said, "don't go into politics".

"Why?" Man Plus asked.

"Because your skirt will be free".

"Are you jealous?" Man Plus asked.

"I will never be jealous, I will never be a jealous husband. Go, join, and you will see that I will never be jealous".

Man Plus continued her campaign. "We will clean the gutters," she said, "we will set up a team of women to properly look after children left in the streets by mothers eking out their living in the market places of our community".

When she heard that one of the reasons girls miss out a lot on schooling was because schools provide no facilities for menstruating girls, she vowed to make sanitary pads an essential school supply.

Because Man Plus wore awareness trousers under her skirt, Madu The Mason mocked her, saying "it is easy for a man to pee while wearing trousers, he will just unzip the flap. But for a woman, she would have to pull down the whole trouser. That's why a man's thing like being a councilor is like trousers, the real thing does not lie in putting them on, it is about having them on and doing our thing".

Man Plus replied, "we will create special pee places for women, so they don't have to go running all around the place looking for suitable places to pull down their trouser without exposing their buttocks to the prying eyes of the public".

Older women loved the facts of her words; youths liked the bravery of her promises. They flocked to her campaign events to hear her speak; they followed her from house to house to make her case for a woman's voice in the councils of decisions.

The incumbent called on his most loyal supporters to intimidate her. They hired the champion cusser to cuss her, the selfsame master-cusser one who defeated Madu The Mason in the cussing match. Man Plus did not quit the race.

The incumbent hired night soil men to throw faeces at her door. Morning when she woke up, she found it difficult to push her door against something stacked against it. She pushed and pushed, and slightly opened the door. Foul winds rushed in, so smelly that she fell backwards. She stood up again, and pushed hard, with the strength of a woman in labour. The door opened to a smelly world of shit and piss. She did not quit the race.

Rather she organised the biggest cleaning operation ever held in the community. They scrubbed the smelly latrines, removing from dark corners some of the dirtiest secrets of the community - ill-disposed condoms and menstrual pads; a two months old aborted foetus, half eaten by some cats; a woman's photo locked inside an old tin and placed behind a latrine box, which an old man said was a way to make the photographed person

70

have a smelly present and a smellier future; wonders of wonders, lots of money wrapped in several layers of plastic seen in another part of the latrine, and later claimed by a woman saying it was money she was hiding from her husband who usually seized money she earned through trading so that he could spend it on bend-elbow and back-on-the-ground. Man Plus and the women also cleaned the gutters, removing weeks old fish entrails in black plastic bags; they scrubbed the favourite piss corners of the men of the community, even digging out the putrid piss-soils and putting in their place soils taken from cleaner places in the community.

The incumbent appealed to the most fearsome secret society, like he did about an opponent the last time, getting that opponent to quit the race after he saw red clothes tied with a string of cowries and hung on his door. An old man warned Man Plus, " that man will kill you, he has the most powerful society on his side; he has hired the wickedest sorcerers to do you harm".

Man Plus did not quit. Rather when they saw some wicked looking charms near her house, she cut one hundred lime and poured the liquid on the wicked charms; then she dug a hole, put the evil charms inside the hole, and gathered forty women to pee on them, before covering them, haphazardly disgracefully, like they did corpses of evil men.

The queues were long on polling day; the day was hot; the heat made the polling officials sweat; the sweat soiled some ballot papers; the soiled papers agitated the polling agents of the candidates; the agitation led to lots of accusation; the accusations led to counter accusation in the polling station - including that some voters were using fake names; that some had voted more than once; that the polling officials were showing illiterate voters the wrong way to vote; and more and more.

Ami Silencer showed up to vote; the accusations and counter accusations stopped as people made way for her to pass through. She voted just ahead of Dulai Free Talk. Their eyes met. The way she walked was now awakening memories of a woman Dulai Free Talk knew during his road construction days. But her face reminded him of his own mother. Ami Silencer smiled and returned to her house. The accusations and counter accusations resumed, and went on until counting time: the woman challenger won by a landslide; the biggest votes of any councilor in the country.

"They say I cannot wear their trouser, that even the strongest man would melt before the fury of the incumbent. Well let me announce to you all; I'm not a man; I'm Man Plus".

Rugie Fry-fry

Rugie Fry-fry's husband, Orman The Artist had great appetite for mammy-and-daddy business, and he took to wooing as many women as he could. Orman The Artist would bring them home whilst Rugie Fry-fry was at the junction selling fry-fry, from around nightfall to midnight.

Not that Rugie Fry-fry did not know about her husband taking women home. Not that it was like some secret that only a few people knew about. Not that other married women had on many occasions not urged her to stop this nonsense. "You are making our married men think it is okay to bring girlfriends home," they told her.

But Rugie Fry-fry only smiled. Just about two years ago, she realised that her husband would only be great with her after he had had mammy-and-daddy business with another women.

The Sage said, "True say talk me,' so let me say the truth, only the heart that loves knows the joys of staying".

The other married women did not even know that Rugie Fry-fry sometimes pushed other women towards her husband. Not directly, but through suggestions. She said to a woman, "hmmm, that my husband, I suspect he spends lots of money on

74

women, but if they hide, why do I need to go looking for them". She said to another, "that my husband, he is so caressingly sweet, but you know, I'm most times busy with my fry-fry. I love his style, he knows how to make a woman happy". She said to an adventurous young woman, "hmmm, you are the type of woman my husband would like; don't go near him o, for if he sees you from around nightfall to mid night when I'm busy here selling my fry-fry, he will fall for you".

True say talk me,' so let me say the truth," said The Sage. "Many wise women have great powers of suggestions as a way to be in control. They would act in suggestive ways to the men they are in love with, and the men would act to woo them; and the foolish man would think he is the one taking the initiative, when in actual fact it is the woman putting grains of rice on the ground for the foolish man-fowl to follow until he gets trapped in the woman's coop".

So it was that Rugie even manipulated women into thinking that it was her man that was wooing them, when actually it was Rugie herself that was wooing them for her man. Even her man thought he was the one doing the wooing. And he would thump his chest amongst his peers, "look, I know how to get women".

So Santigie Ginger Da Fitter asked Orman to help him woo a woman. Orman went to the woman's house and said, "I want you to leave your boyfriend for my handsome friend, Santigie Ginger Da Fitter".

The woman asked, "Do we eat handsomeness?"

He answered, "Not only that, he's a fool, he will share everything with you".

"What!"

Orman continued, "a handsome fool man is good husband material. His handsomeness will make you feel good, and his stupidity will give you three things: it will make you control him, it will make you laugh, and he will not be able to cheat on you, for he can make no good story to hide his cheating".

The woman replied, "I don't want a fool for a husband".

Orman tried three other times to woo women for his friends. He told the first woman, "my friend is rich; he will take care of you; and you will be as bellyful as a thief's wife".

This directness angered the woman, "get out of my house," she shouted. "I don't want to be a thief's wife. I'm not one of those women who cannot take care of themselves. I go and come everyday. Even when things are tough, I go and come; walking for nothing is better than sitting down for nothing. I don't sit by myself waiting for a man to rescue me. I can take care of my self, get out".

The other time he was so clumsy that the woman threw at him water she had just used to clean her plates. Peppery water in his eyes, he could not properly see the gutter and his shin hit the gutter's edge, and he shouted, "Pepper, pepper, pepper in my eyes, pepper on my foot".

The third woman Orman tried to woo for his friend went to Rugie Fry-fry, "Warn your husband," she said, " I'm not a foolish woman".

"So only foolish women want my husband, so I am a foolish woman?"

"Don't build a house on my mouth, I did not say that. I said I am not a foolish woman. Your husband came to me to woo me for his friend. Tell him I am not cheap".

Rugie Fry-fry was very annoyed with her man for this. "What," she said to Orman, "foolish man, so you are now a hired wooer for other men?"

Rugie Fry-fry had never been so annoyed with him like this. He asked for forgiveness, "I will never woo women for friends again".

"Better"" said Rugie Fry-fry, "if you must be blamed, be blamed for women you woo for yourself. Don't go tote cusses for other people for nothing".

Orman's friends laughed at him, "men who apologise to women for having other women are weak men. With all the big mouth you have been making about being in control of your wife, look at how you trembled before her".

But Orman kept his promise to Rugie Fry-fry; he stopped trying to woo women for his friends. He said to Dulai Free Talk, "I think I'm better at wooing women for myself than wooing them for others".

Ami Silencer, who everyone thought was The Wife of The Poda Poda Driver heard him say this; she smiled, and continued her way. Dulai Free Talk looked at the way she smiled and said to himself, "I feel some connection to this woman. Her smiles are now reminding me of Sallay during my road construction days. But sure, she could not be Sallay. Sallay was just a little younger than I was. She should be old enough be Ami Silencer's mother.

"True say talk me," said The Sage, "the differences in human faces and behaviors are not so great. That's why we often meet people who remind us of others. We resemble each other a lot".

Rugie Fry-fry continued to push them unto him. Most times she would even give these women her fry-fry so that they could eat well before going to her husband.

One day her friend, Dama, The Wife of Orfi Usu The Policeman scolded her, 'you are a fool; the woman you are so good to is your husband's lover?'

"I know, but leave them alone".

"What, are you afraid?"

"Of course you know I am not".

"If you can't, please let me do unto them what you did unto the women who were my husband's lover".

Rugie Fry-fry laughed, remembering how the two of them launched a campaign against the women they suspected of dating Dama's husband. Some of them were easily scared off, especially those who were a bit older, who were born in ages past when dating married men was considered an unbecoming behaviour that must be hidden.

But not so a young woman down the other road. She would not budge. She boasted, "we are all rivals now, I date your man, somebody else is dating my man and you may be dating that person's man".

Rugie Fry-fry and Dama rushed at her with frying spoons. The young woman and her friends held up pot covers as shields. The neighbourhood gathered around the spectacle of frying spoons as swords and pot covers as shields. Older women supported

Rugie Fry-fry and Dama; they were surprised at the younger women who were openly boasting and fighting for men that were not their husbands. But the younger women said, "go deal with your husband, your contract is with him, not us; we had no contract with you, so we did not break any contract with you". And there was a third group of women who shook their heads in disgust at the fighting women and their supporters. "Men are not worth fighting for," they said.

"But men fight for us; they even kill for us," said an old woman who ran away from a war in the late 60s and settled in our community. "My first love was killed during the war by a man who wanted me. I did not in fact know he wanted me. He asked me, "who is your man? He's very lucky to have you, I want to congratulate him for knowing how to pick a beautiful woman". When I showed him my man, he shot him dead and tried to run away with me. Another man shot him dead. "You are too bad," he said to the dead killer. So you see, two men died over me. The man who shot the man who shot my man became my protector during the war. He never said he wanted me. But one day another woman came in and slapped me, "so you are the one preventing my man from giving me his attention". I fought back, someone just couldn't slap me for a man and I sit there saying "hmmm, men are not worth fighting for". In fact, after that fight, I told the man, "I love you". He replied, "what!" But I told him, "one can't just be slapped for nothing, let me at least enjoy what I was slapped for".

Ami Silencer, who everybody thought was The Wife of The Poda Poda Driver heard all this from inside her room. She smiled and lay backwards on the bed. Dulai Free Talk was at the junction of the quarrels, making faces at the women.

That fight between married women and unmarried women was months ago. But standing before Rugie Fry-fry at the junction and seeing how she was not giving a damn about Orman's affairs, Dama asked her, "so you too have joined those women who think men are not worth fighting for?"

"Leave them alone," Rugie Fry-fry Woman shouted.

"Leave them alone," I said quietly, "reasons for certain actions are lots of time only understood by those who do them".

Of course they did not hear me say that. But believe me, I was listening to their conversations. Don't you ever think I am telling a lie, like those other story tellers do. I hate lies, so the conversation between those two women that I am telling you about is true. They were having their talk at the main junction of our area where Rugie Fry-fry sold her fry-fry.

That junction was everybody's sitting room. Rugie Fry-fry and her friend did not pay any attention to me as they spoke; for if you paid undue attention to the many mouths of the junction you wouldn't be able to say a thing, and not saying a thing would make your mouth smelly, and the stories of your life would rot inside you. I was sitting on my favourite sitting place - the topmost rung of steps that once led to a room of the house burnt down by petrol hoarded during a petrol shortage in our area. So the steps, like some stories, now led nowhere. Believe me, I saw that house burning. A friend of the owner of the room not knowing there was petrol under the bed struck a match whilst waiting for her girlfriend. Fire engulfed him, engulfed the room and engulfed the whole house.

"Serves them right," said The Ladani, "that's a foretaste of the hell in which these fornicators will burn".

The Old Imam admonished him, " don't say that, Ladani; in times of tragedy you pray for the victim not blame them; hell is not something a good person should wish for somebody's soul".

"I'm sorry, Imam, may God have mercy on them".

82

That room in that burnt out house was one of the several joy-rooms in our area. So you want to know about joy rooms? Okay let me tell you:

You are a young man capable of mammy-and-daddy business. You are now tired of sleeping with a dozen relatives on the floor of the parlour of your uncle's place. Somewhere you hear a room is being rented out. A married man with some spare cash says to you, "young man, I am going to rent that room for you, and I will put some strong bed therein. Make sure the bed remains strong for I would be coming with women to test the strength of the bed". Another man, seeing that you now have a whole room to yourself starts giving you little cash once in a while. Another adulterer always buys you fry-fry from Rugie Fry-fry and says, "take this for yourself, take this other one to your room, I am expecting a visitor there". Your room is now a joy-room and you now live off the joys taking place in your room.

But let us leave this story about joy rooms and continue with our story of Rugie Fry-fry. Rugie Fry-fry's fry-fry found favour with folks. Food fans frequented from far and farther for their favourite fry-fry —fried fish, fried potatoes, fried beef and boiled kanda dipped in hot pepper and onions. Only her husband, Orman did not seem to like her fry-

83

fry. He always invoked the old saying to her: eaters should know that the loud sounds of frying, or the sweet smells of cooking do not make food delicious. Sometimes the nastiest foods make the loudest sounds and give out the sweetest smells.

Dama continued to ask Rugie, "why must you be so docile with your husband? Look at how he is describing your fry-fry. He wants to spoil your way with your customers".

"Not everything should be taken seriously, many things are jokes; it's his way of joking with me".

And Rugie Fry-fry also told Dama, "The Ladani said we must find heaven at the foot of our husbands".

Dama replied, "impossible, The Ladani really does not know how smelly my husbands feet are, else he won't advise me to look for heaven between those smell-smell toes. The toes are so packed together that the areas between them are always so damp and smelly. Oh God let me don't find heaven between those toes that stink like a piss pool newly disturbed after being still for years".

Rugie Fry-fry said, "with such descriptions of your husband, no wonder you always fight".

"No no no," Dama laughed, "you should have said, "no wonder you always beat up your useless husband"".

"I would not say that about my friend's husband".

"But he is useless, always drunk, all of his squad mates have gained lots of promotion in the Police Force. But his drunkenness would not allow him to be promoted".

"You want some fry-fry?" Rugie Fry-fry asked Dama.

"You want to change the topic eh?"

"Oh typical Salone person; you never answer a question".

"Alright, alright, I don't want you to pull Salone's story out of my mouth. Let me have some fry-fry".

"When are you going to pay for it?" Rugie Fry-fry asked.

"I'm not your only debtor. The Ladani owes you money; Asi owes you; Madu The Mason owes you; Shekuna The Poda Poda Driver owes you; Kama Bluffer owes you; Santigie Ginger owes you; Sorie Measurement owes you; Momoh The Corpse Washer owes you; even Mamatu Cookery, who everybody owes, also owes you".

'True say talk me,' so I say the truth," said The Sage, "debtors live long, for creditors pray for them not to get sick or die".

"That's why my business is not growing, too many people owe me. I must stop giving credit; the

85

stories are too much. This would say, "I was about to come and pay you, but my baby girl fell sick". This other one would say, "The one who owes me money has not yet paid me". That other one would say, "I am going to my cousin who just returned from overseas, I will pay you the soonest I return from the visit". Too many stories in this place, too many stories; but do we eat stories? Tell me Dama, is it stories that we eat?"

The Teacher-writer

"Spell 'teacher,'" The Teacher-writer asked a pupil in his Form Two class.

"T-i-c-h-a," the pupil spelled.

The Teacher-writer called another pupil, "spell serious".

"S-e-a-r-i-u-s," the pupil called out, lingering a little on each of the letters in his spelling.

He called another, and another, and another - fifty students in all; almost half his class. None of the pupils gave the correct spellings. His patience ran out, and he shouted, "these are spellings you should have learned to spell in primary school".

Everywhere he turned in the community, The Teacher-writer saw a plague of bad spellings. The plague had been following him like some bad smell, first in small wafts, and then with full force; like how little drops of piss makes trousers smelly and gets the owner to do something about it. So he decided to organise some extra lessons where he would teach his student the basics of spelling.

"That would be fine," said the Head of the English Department of the school. "How much would you be charging for the extra lessons? You know the policy here, 40% of the lesson fee comes to the department for administrative and developmental activities".

"I want to do it for free," the Teacher-writer replied.

"What, are you mad? Do you know how much money you would be throwing away? I will not allow it".

The Head of Department tried to scuttle the initiative. But the Principal told him, "no man, this is too much. Let there be some areas where money should not be the consideration".

The Teacher-writer started the extra lessons at school. He was very tough against misspellings during these lessons. Some days he would get misspelling children to kneel down with hands up in the air for hours; other days he would get them to bend towards the ground with their index fingers touching the floor, and one leg raised; other times he would let them gather their fingertips together and he would hit the gathered fingertips with wooden rulers. When a new teacher once asked him why he would punish the children so harshly, he replied, "We need to catch them young; no spelling should be left behind".

The new teacher said corporal punishment was against human rights, that it did not not improve learning.

The Teacher-writer replied, "it is this human rights thing that is responsible for all this. Everything is human rights, human rights. The other day a mother came here, telling me I should not beat her child. I told her, "be gone woman, you may pamper your child at home, but I won't pamper him here". The woman removed her child from school. Can you imagine that, she removed him from school rather than make us discipline the child. What is this world coming to?"

The new teacher said, "the bodies of people are not drums to beat. If you want sad music buy a real drum and turn your own voice into the cries you love to hear".

"Who told you I love sad music? Who told you I'm a sadist?" The Teacher-writer asked. "I beat them for their own sake, that they do not become thugs and thieves and ravishers of people".

The new teacher answered, "If we want a less violent community we should start by not beating those who are close to us".

It was a big argument at the school that day, with the older teachers laughing at the lack of backbones by the younger teachers; and the younger teacher talking about the meanness of the older teachers.

"It was that meanness that got you educated," said an older teacher.

"But how did it get to this point, if you were so good, how did it come to this? How did you come to holler at us for lacking backbones; was it that your beatings broke backbones?"

The Teacher-writer continued his beating ways at the school. But what should he do about the wider community? He certainly could not beat up the people into spelling well. So what should he do about the signs of the community? He saw poor spellings on signposts – *Kamara and Suns; Jalloh and Brodas; Pipull Famicy, We Cell all Types of Drogs*. He saw poor spellings on the back, front and sides of vehicles – *To bi A Man is not Ezi; Murder's Blessing; The Dawn Fowl of a Man is Not the Endin of His Life; God Bles the Owna.* He saw bad spellings on lists of items- *pam oil, burta, casava lifs, solt.* It was as if he only had eyes for them. He would jump over correct spellings without praising their correctness, only to be stuck at a wrong spelling that came after a hundred words, or two hundred words, or two thousand words. He would stand there shaking his head, "oh God, oh God, why should this country be inflicted with this plague. What has this land done wrong to deserve this?"

"Truth says, 'say me,' so let me say the truth," said The Sage, "wrongness is louder than correctness. You would do the correct thing all your days, but a single wrong thing may be what people remember about you".

"I must do more about this plague of bad spellings," The Teacher-writer promised. So? He learnt how to paint letters to stop the plague of bad spellings. His problem, however, was that he knew the theories of painting more than he knew how to paint. So? He spelt well but painted badly. And many people cared more about how the painting was beautiful than about how it was wise. So? Many avoided him; and he could not get those who could paint well to come to him because these guys did not want to give him a share of their earnings.

The other day he went to the artist, Orman, the husband of Rugie Fry-fry and said to him, "let's come together Orman, with your beauty and my wisdom, we will conquer all".

Orman looked at him like a man who had won the heart of a woman would regard another man who had failed to snatch his love but now came with a proposal on how to hold on to that woman.

"Why are you looking at me like that?" The Teacher-writer asked.

"I don't need your wisdom, teacher," Orman said. "beauty is better than wisdom".

This angered The Teacher-writer, and he said, "what do you know about betterment? You fool, you body without brain, you form without substance".

Orman replied, "look at your life, teacher. Your shoes are as bent as the lines behind your trousers showing the divide between the two lobes of your oblong waist. I am sure the tailor who sewed your trousers could not have sewn those bent lines. So the lines are bent because your waist is bent. So as an artist, let me advise you: allow your shirt to flow over your waist, don't tuck your shirt inside your trousers. Your belt is like some bush rope and your waist is more bent than a bush path".

Ami Silencer, who everybody thought was the wife of The Poda Poda Driver was passing by, it was about this time that The Poda Poda Driver usually returned from work. She smiled and continued her way. Dulai Free Talk watched her as she passed by; his eyes followed her, "the way she walks, she way she walks, like a combination of the way Sallay and my mother walked. I just can't figure it out, I just can't figure it out".

The other time The Teacher-writer saw the date of somebody on his birth certificate written as "the turd of match 1979".

One day The Ladani asked The Teacher-writer to repaint the signs against pissing and throwing rubbish against the foundation of the house The

Ladani was staying. People hardly paid attention to the crumbling writings. Rather they pissed on them; they threw rubbish at them. The Ladani told The Teacher writer, "the piss, especially the strong piss of men are eating into the foundation, destroying it. Please re-paint the signs bold and clear".

The Teacher- writer felt very bad about the signs -'do not peace here,' 'do not throw rob bush here'. He said the bad spellings were communicating badly and people were not paying heed to the writings because of that.

It was almost night when The Teacher-writer started the work and the drunken man did not see The Teacher-writer bent low by the gutter to correct and repaint the signs. The Teacher-writer felt warm liquid on the skin covering his spine. He turned, "what, you are pissing on me".

"Sorry, so sorry," said the pissing man, who continued pissing, only that this time he was pissing on the writings.

"What," said The Teacher-writer, "you are pissing on the writings telling you not to piss here".

The pissing man looked at The Teacher-writer like a photographer would a negative that he had raised unto some dim light to see its contours better, "only a fool would think mere writings could tie up the piss bags of a man like me".

The Teacher-writer shook his head, "this is just confirming this statement for me - you know how developed a place is by what they use their gutters for. If the gutters are only for carrying rainwater away from the city and wastewater away from dwellings, it is a developed place. Where the gutter is for pissing and throwing rubbish, and for sitting over to eat and discuss, then that place is a slum, uncouth, and uncivil".

"Nonsense," said the pisser, "so you want me to piss on my trouser, you want us to hide to eat, you want us to paint gutters with fine-fine English as you are doing now?"

"You pissed on me and my writing, and you stand here talking nonsense".

"To hell with your writings," said the pisser, "we will piss on them if they are in our gutters talking about our gutters".

Orfi Usu The Police Man

Everybody in the community knew that Orfi Usu's wife beat him up when he got drunk. Well, everybody knew that except Orfi Usu himself, and even when we told him that the bruises on his body were the fingernail marks of Dama, his wife, he denied it.

"No," he told us, "don't you see how my wife defends me, don't you see how she loves me, don't you see how she bathes my wounds like a grandmother bathes her baby-grandchild, slowly, singing songs that come from the belly of her joys?"

Orfi Usu was a squad mate of some of the most senior officers in the Force. But he had never gotten beyond sergeant. Well, he did get beyond it once, but his misbehaviour got him demoted to sergeant, then to corporal, and then to private again.

His senior colleagues had a soft spot for him. They say he saved about eight of them from being expelled from the Police Training School during their recruit days. They had gone out at night, nine of them, including Orfi Usu himself, to a nightclub. They were not supposed to do that. But they were young and wanted a break from the rigours of the school. A fight broke out at the nightclub. The squad of nine stood together and beat up a gang of rowdy youths. One of these youths was the son of a big man in the country. The recruits left the scene, but Orfi Usu was caught. They asked him about the squad that was with him. He denied it, saying he alone did everything that was done; that he alone beat up the gang of the son of the big man; that he alone cussed his father; that he also said he did not care about the consequences. He was detained for one week; he did not change his story. They scorched his thing with the lit ends of cigarettes, because they knew he would not show his thing to be photographed as evidence of torture; he did not change his stories.

The Sage said, "truth says, 'say me,' so let me say the truth, there are no stories that could not be changed; but if you want your story to gather truth along the way, stick to it, don't change it, even though it was originally made up. But most stories, anyway, are made up".

They tortured Orfi Usu to reveal the other names. He did not. In the end the big man grew fond of him on account of his loyalty and got him released and sent back to the training school. They say the beatings he got whilst in the cells changed him. He was tormented. He became a drunkard.

That was a long time ago, when they say the police did not care much about human rights; when you might see the police with those big sticks they called *koboko* that they would use so often; when the police would be seen beating and dragging suspects along the muds of the land; when they would lock people up for weeks for delaying to pay debts owed to the in-law of the cousin of the girlfriend of a constable. But Orfi Usu said the too much human rights thing was making people misbehave a lot; he blamed the increases in crime to this talk of human rights and democracy.

Like that thief he was demoted for because he did not stop people of the community from beating him mercilessly. The thief dressed like a woman, with frock and wig and false breasts and waist. There was blackout. He sneaked into the house. He was going into a room when lights came on again. Residents asked him, where he was going. He stepped back, and started running. In a corner he removed his frock and all the false things about him. But they caught him anyway. A little boy saw him and pointed it out.

"He is a witch," said the little boy. "I saw him transforming himself from a woman to a man".

The thief trembled; he was very afraid. He knew how witches were treated here. One such witch, a man they saw with long breasts was accused of transforming himself into an evil woman; and then back again into an innocent man to prevent people from knowing what he was. They say they caught him in the act of transforming back into a man, but his breasts could not be transformed into a man's because of a spell that had been cast by a woman whose only son had been bewitched into failing his exams and then gambling and then becoming a drug addict. The man with the long breasts was stripped naked and paraded along the streets, a rope tied round the right breast like they did the neck of a goat. But they tied the breast so tight that it came off as if cut by a knife. The man groaned in pain, but they kicked and punched and did a thousand other things unto him.

The thief knew about that murdering of a witch. So when the little boy hollered that he was a witch that had just transformed himself from a woman into a man, he shouted, "no, I'm not a witch, I'm a thief. In fact I'm the biggest thief around. Yesterday, I stole the dozen white knickers The Ladani left in the sun to dry. The day before yesterday I stole five eggs that Rugie Fry-fry's hen laid. Last Wednesday I led a gang of thief to threaten the JC who we thought came from America with lot of dollars to our community. He had no dollars, so we beat him up for being a careless JC. Last Monday I attacked a woman with a knife and took her handbag. Last

Tuesday I stole the shoes that Amadu the Student left to dry on top of their broken fence and sold it as wet as it was at the night market near the police station. Two Fridays ago, I stole the slippers of The Old Imam at the mosque. I was the one who used a long stick to winch out of the window the bag containing the money of Mamatu Cookery. It was I who went to Amy Silencer's place. I met her sitting on their couch, eyes closed. I took some very beautiful clothes from her box. They were the most beautiful clothes I had ever seen, I was transfixed by their beauty. Some noise made Ami Silencer open her eyes. Our eyes met. She smiled, said nothing, and closed her eyes again. I put the clothes down where I met them. I took nothing away, ask her I was the thief that took nothing away from her. I am a thief, not a witch".

A crowd gathered and eight men - two at each foot and each hand - stretched him and each of those he had stolen from came forward and gave him a hundred lashes each. Well all came forward to lash him, except Ami Silencer. The soonest the thief got to the story of Mamatu Cookery's bag, the crowd got especially loud and angry, and did not hear the story of Ami Silencer.

"True say talk me, so let me say the truth, until the ears are prepared for them, some stories cannot be heard".

They beat up the thief especially hard for stealing the bag of Mamatu Cookery. "What," they said, "so you deprived us of the great food of Mamatu Cookery for a week, leaving us to starve every morning for a week".

Orfi Usu was there, laughing in his drunken stupor. In a lull in the beatings the thief ran, and made it to the police station. A human rights woman was visiting the station and she wrote a damning report about the brutality. The police took action and put all the blame on Orfi Usu, and demoted him as punishment. The human rights woman wrote a report, saying how her actions were saving thieves all over the town.

When Orfi Usu was returning with the news of his demotion that day, he met Ami Silencer going to where she usually waited for The Poda Poda Driver. Dulai Free Talk was on the other side of the road watching Ami Silencer but without Ami Silencer knowing he was watching her. He was holding a book on resemblances he had bought on the cheap from a second hand book seller. The book on resemblances had been with the bookseller for while, and no body showed interest in buying it. He had been planning on giving it away to groundnut sellers to wrap their groundnuts when Dulai Free Talk showed up and took the book off the ground near the gutter where the books were displayed. He flipped through it, and asked the bookseller, "where did you get this book?" The bookseller replied, "from a drug addicted son of a professor, he told me I should buy that useless book together with the good books he came with".

Orfi Usu looked at Dulai Free Talk and laughed, "so you still read books?"

"No" Dulai Free Talk back-talked, "these are police statements full of bad stories about people who resemble you".

Orfi Usu continued his way home. Home, he told Dama, his wife, "I have been demoted because of a thief".

Dama slapped his drunken jaw a dozen times. "Drunkard, drunkard, good for nothing man," she cried. A female cousin of Dama came over to help her cuss her man. "Shut up," Dama told her cousin, "who gave you permission to cuss my husband?" And she pushed her cousin to the ground, and the drunken Orfi Usu teamed up with her to beat up the cousin. The cousin grabbed Orfi Usu, and pulled him towards the floor. Orfi Usu fell on top of the cousin, full length on her, head on head, chest on

101

chest, loin on loin, leg on leg. The wife became jealous and tried to yank him off his cousin. "What are you doing, you good for nothing man, don't you know you should not lie on my cousin like you are doing now". But the cousin would not get him get off. She tied her feet round Orfi Usu's waist, and held him tight with her arms. Orfi Usu yelled, "oh this is good, this is heaven, this is good".

Santigie Ginger Da Fitter

That was how the police called him in the public notice announcing his disappearance: Santigie Ginger Da Fitter – *Santigie is a ginger, which is the local word for a person who is almost an albino. He has ginger-coloured hair, dull eyes, red-red lips, broad shoulders, hairy chest, and firm legs. He used to work as a fitter. He disappeared almost forty days ago. He could not be found in any of his usual haunts.*

Santigie Ginger Da Fitter was a man whom people in our community knew much about. They say two years, three weeks and five days after his father and mother divorced, Santigie Ginger said to his mother, "Mama, I know you have been working very hard to pay my school fees and buy my books. But Mama, my head was not created to carry books. Stop wasting your money on my schooling, Mama. Let me go do some other thing".

Santigie's mother had always suspected that her son was a fool, just like his father, who though the handsomest man in her youth turned out to be the idlest, stupidest and laziest man in the community. She had, however, clung to some hope that her son would somehow be different

"True say talk me, so let me say the truth," said The Sage, "what do you expect of his mother? A

103

mother's love, like a lover's love, is like prayers for miraculous healing of a person whose head had been smashed in a motor accident. The prayer convinces you that you are doing something; it makes you feel better when in actuality it cannot stop the death of the smashed-brained person".

"You are so much like your father when your father was your age, you are truly your father's son," Santigie Ginger's mother told him.

Santigie Ginger smiled, "oh Mama, oh Mama, I have seen the pictures; Papa was so handsome. So I am like him? Oh wonderful. I hope a woman as beautiful as you are will marry me".

"Fool," said his mother, "you've finally turned out to be no better than your father; he was so stupid. I had thought you would be as good as me, but oh no, oh no; you have grown up to become like him".

The next day, Santigie Ginger's mother went to the head of the Motor Mechanic Garage in our community and asked him to take on her son as a trainee. The Head Fitter, an old man who had been in that position for so long that no body remembered how long said, "you've done well; maybe he'll do better at learning the trade than his father. His father took five years learning to work on engines; nothing. He took three years to learn how to spray; nothing. Four years learning to be a motor electrician; nothing. And two years to be a panel beater; nothing. One day I asked him, "is your head so strong like rocks that nothing enters it?" He replied, "I think so, don't you see when I fight, I crack skulls with my head butts".

"That was why I left him," Santigie Ginger's mother said. "He uses his forehead on everything. You won't believe it, one day because some rascals bet he would not do it, he used his forehead to crack-open a coconut. The other time, we mistakenly locked our keys inside our room; before I knew it, he used his forehead on the door; one butt and the door broke open".

When they asked Santigie Ginger which of the trades of the garage he would love to learn, he answered, "panel beating".

A month into the training, Santigie Ginger's mother came running to the garage, "Santigie has killed me, Santigie has killed me".

"What happened?" the Head Fitter asked

"Did you tell him to do what he did?" Santigie Ginger's mother shouted. "Did you?"

"I don't know what happened; how would I know whether I told him to do what he did or not?"

"I met him denting my pans and plates. When I asked him what he was doing; he said he was doing his homework, that his garage boss told him to find dented pans and practice how to return the pans to their original condition by using the skills they are learning. I met two plates completely damaged; two other plates that had already been heated and hammered. He was putting polyfilla on them, and shine-papering them".

The Old Fitter laughed hard and long, "just like his father, just like his father. I remember when they were teaching him about fixing the under-carriage of vehicles and his boss told him to train his eyes to see in the darkness underneath the vehicles. He went home one weekend and stayed under bed all day long. When his father asked him what he was doing under the bed, he answered, "I am training my eyes to see the underneath of things".

Santigie Ginger continued to dent his mother's pans, and then pots. And then he moved on to the pans, pots and plates of relatives, and then unto those of neighbours. He would dent, hammer softly to get them back to shape and put polyfilla on them, just like he did unto his mother's.

Santigie Ginger's mother led one begging-for-forgiveness mission after another to neighbours until the leader of those missions, The Ladani got tired and fled anytime he saw her.

"I'm tired of leading begging missions," The Ladani told Orfi Usu, his next-door neighbour. "Every day every time people come here to get me to lead begging missions. A man slapped the wife of another; they would come to me, "Ladani, please lead a begging mission to the husband and wife". A woman who plaited her hair with expensive false-hair but could not pay some debt less expensive than the hair, would come to me, "Ladani, please lead a begging mission for me to the by-day woman". The person who has failed to pay her dues to the Osusu group would come to me, "Ladani please lead a begging mission for me to the Osusu master". The mother of the youth who impregnated the schoolgirl came to me, "Ladani, please lead a begging mission for me to the father of the schoolgirl". The sister of the young boy who was playing football in the street and smashed the glass window of the neighbour with his foolish ball would come to me, "Ladani, please lead a begging mission for me to the window owner". The other day, the brother of a thief who stole the knickers of a women left to dry at the back of the house came to me and said, "Ladani, please lead a begging mission for me to the owners of the knickers". "What!" I shouted, "me, go beg for knickers?" Another day, the man cussing every morning at the junction came to me, "Ladani, I heard that Mammy Haja heard my bad words; I so respect her, please lead a begging mission for me to her". Two days later he cussed again and came back to me, "Mammy Haja again heard my bad words, please lead a begging mission for me to her". He came after he had cussed again, and came again, and again, and again. The other day, the mother of a boy who dirtied the clothes of Ami Silencer with his ball came to me and said, "Ladani, please lead a begging mission for me to Ami Silencer". We met her sitting in their veranda looking far into space. We asked for forgiveness. She smiled, said nothing, moved her hands to indicate that what the boy did meant nothing to her, and then walked into her place. One day, I was not even on a begging mission, when Orbangu, on seeing me coming down the road hollered, "I will not accept any begging from people o, I will not accept any begging from people, now that the boys are playing *botkidi* near my glass window, no body is warning them o. I will not take no begging o and left with the loss of dealing with it. This is wickedness, this is wickedness, this begging-begging is making people irresponsible, this begging-begging is too much o. I will not take begging o, even if they gather all the holy men of the land to come meet me, I will not take any begging from anyone".

So it was that The Ladani himself started running away from begging missions; so it was that he fled anytime he saw Santigie Ginger's mother coming with a plea for him to lead a begging mission.

But what made everyone give up on the stupidity of Santigie Ginger was when in the cussing competition with cuss-cuss teacher, Dulai Free Talk he commenced his cussing by first cussing his own mother a hundred and one times in about three minutes and forty-seven seconds.

Santigie Ginger's mother got so tired of the troubles his son's stupidity wrought upon her that she stood naked in the dead of the night at the junction and put a curse on those responsible: "Today, as naked I was born, in the presence of your darkness, I ask you to destroy those responsible for my son's stupidity. If it is your will, let it be your will. But if it is someone gathering the little stupidities of the world to flood my son's head, push it back unto them, make them stupider than the total stupidity of forty persons each of whom is forty times stupider than my son".

The curse seemed to have no impact. Santigie Ginger continued to do stupider things. In fact people ascribed so many stupid things to him that we began to doubt whether all these talk of his stupidity were true. Like when they said Santigie

Ginger's boss asked him to put some stone behind the wheels of a vehicle whose engines he was about to start to check how its steering wheel worked. Santigie Ginger used a very small stone. Whereupon the boss shouted, "such a small stone, Santigie Ginger, why would you use such a small stone to stop the vehicle? Learn to use your head, Santigie Ginger, use your head". Santigie Ginger removed the small stone, lay flat on the floor and put his head against the back tire. "What!" the boss man hollered, "you want to give me trouble, you want to give me trouble".

Like this other story of Santigie Ginger being asked to bring an 18 spanner. He took a long time at the toolbox. The boss asked, "Santigie Ginger, what is taking you so long?" He replied, "the spanners are not up to 18 sir, I have only seen about nine spanners".

One day, The Old Fitter told us "why is it that so many people send their stubborn stupid relatives to learn my trade, as if this is a stupid profession. This relative would come, "my son refuses to go to school, please train him to become a fitter". This other one would come, "my son has been failing his examinations every time, please train him to become a panel beater". "My son is very stubborn at home, please train him to be a spray man". No this is a life saving profession, lives of people depend on good vehicles, good business depend on good vehicles, but some of these stupid boys, some of these stupidly stubborn boys, they are making life very difficult for all of us".

But when we asked why he never turned them away, he said, "you never know how they would turn out to be. Look at Santigie Ginger, who would think he would marry such a beautiful young woman with so much money. Now look at these great tools he bought for me, look at the vehicle maintenance contract he has brought for this garage, would he have done this if I ..."

A trainee ran in hollering, "Santigie Ginger has disappeared, Santigie Ginger has disappeared, ask the radio, ask the radio, he has not been seen for over forty days".

The Old Fitter was so startled that he choked on his words, "no, no, no, that's not the way to give bad news, that's not the way".

And then he cried bitterly, for he remembered that in his long life, he had heard about seven disappearances of albinos, and none had ever returned.

Ami Silencer, who everyone thought was the wife of The Poda Poda Driver saw him cry. She shook her head and went her way. Dulai Free Talk said to himself, "the way this Ami Woman shakes her head is too very familiar. I just feel connected to her somehow. But perhaps, there is no connection, perhaps the resemblances just confirm what the book on resemblances says about resemblances - perhaps it is just that, that because our physical and other traits are not very different, one always sees people that remind you of other people you know. Perhaps this is the case, this is the case with Ami Silencer".

Dulai Free Talk

Dulai Free Talk looked at himself in a mirror and said, "Lordamasi, look at how ugly I am: big mouth, bulging eyes and rugged forehead, huge torso, frog-like belly, hen-like waist, and knee-caps as protruding as a pregnancy of eight-months. My skin looks like it is sewn too tight for my body, no wonder I walk like one with tight fitting trousers, but who should nonetheless move fast, else, he would miss out on some thing he likes very much".

Dulai Free Talk told his man-man, Orman The Artist, "I'm not made for serious things, I'm made to be laughed at. But who is it that could not be laughed at".

Dulai Free Talk was a masquerade maker in his teens, he would tell his peers, you are responsible for stealing your father's socks, you will bring your mother's wedding gloves, you your sister's shine-shine skirt. One day the adults converged on his child-masquerade, yanking off their stolen things, and leaving the teen wearing the masquerade down to his pants. Behold-behold, he was the son of The Old Imam.

Dulai Free Talk told The Old Imam, "as you can see sir, your son was the only one amongst us who nobody would thought of as being the one inside the masquerade. He loves masquerades, but out of respect for you, we didn't want people to see him dancing openly, that would give you a bad name. So we put him inside the masquerade to *soutoura* your honour, but these people, these people, they have disgraced both our secret society and our imam".

The Old Imam shook his head and left the scene.

Dulai Free Talk would be seen after a good meal at Mamatu's Cookery shop pulling up his clothes to rub his stomach, "when I'm hungry, I remember my mother, but when I'm bellyful I say, it was great that she died".

He told The Teacher-writer, "you are a bad man, that's why you like to beat children. Were you clever at school? We were in the same class, and you were both the oldest and the stupidest. But I hear you now tell your students about how clever you were, that you always came first in class, nonsense".

"Truth says 'say me,' so let me say the truth. Which teacher is there who would say he was not serious in school?" The Sage asked. "No way it is in their job to talk about serious students, even if that means making up stories of how serious they the teachers were when they were students".

They say Dulai Free Talk had been like that since he learned to talk, saying things in ways others would not say them. They say he was brilliant at school, and that his father was a seaman. His father went to sea one day and never returned. 'That's how albinos end," said the old man, "they don't die, they just disappear". His mother, a fishmonger worked very hard to keep him in school.

"She died young, his mother," said the old woman. "It was during some heavy rains. Rainwater flooded the streets. She was returning from the market. There was some hole in the covered footpath; the slab covering that part of the footpath had been removed a few days back so that some workers would remove silt and dirt from the gutter. She did not know the hole was there. She fell into the big gutter and got carried away to the sea. Her remains were never found".

But Dulai Free Talk gave a foolish reason for his mother death. "She missed her husband, she's gone to find him at sea so she could cook for him".

The new man of God proclaimed it the work of the river spirits called *mammy wata*. He said, "this place was called The Wailing Places on account of its many *mammy wata* that got people to drown, to wail as they drowned, and for the relatives to wail louder at the loss of their kinfolks to the water spirit. But the missionaries of early Freetown had tied this water spirit with Governor Clarkson's Prayers and expelled her from the place. But now, because you people refused to give your due reverence to the true God, the water spirits are back again, rushing in with stones and rocks and dirt filled evil water from the hills to sweep people into the sea".

Dulai Free Talk laughed, "nonsense, the waters are rushing at us because we have cut down the trees that would have slowed their progress down the hills; the silt are filling the gutters because we have made skinheads of the mountains; and the dirt are the garbage we throw into the gutters".

"You leave no one and situation untouched by your foolishness," Orman The Artist told Dulai Free Talk.

Dulai Free Talk's mother died just after Dulai Free Talk had taken his GCE and filled his applications form for the university. He got very good results. His good results got him accepted. He started a term at the university but could not continue as there was no one to pay his fees. It was during that one term in college that he heard the news of albinos being killed in some far away land for body parts to make good luck charms. "Perhaps," he said to himself "perhaps what my mother told me was true, perhaps my father did not just disappear, perhaps this practice is here but hidden by the story that albinos disappear rather than die".

People called him Dulai Lie Lie College on account of his spending only one term at the university. But that name did not last long. The stories of his free talk and backtalk were stronger than the story of his college.

"True say talk me, so let me say the truth, this place likes funny story more than sad stories," said The Sage. "Even where the story is sad, they often say it in funny ways".

"Carelessness", Dulai Free Talk also said of his mother, "rather than wait for me to go through college, she decided to die; now there is no college for me".

That was long ago, they say, before even The Ladani found religion in our region. Dulai Free Talk was The Ladani's cousin, and The Ladani stayed with them when he first arrived in our region.

"We used to sleep together, this Ladani," said Dulai Free Talk. "I know him left and right, up and down. They say when he was little boy upcountry, he used to tie his leg to the leg of the table, so that when the elders woke up early in the morning to eat during Ramadan, the table's movement would wake him up. He later became a criminal running away from justice, and his mother aided and abetted him. That my aunty, they say his poor husband, a hunter, having not eaten for days woke up one day and told

117

my aunty and the hungry family that he had a dream. He said, "in my dream today, I killed a huge animal". My aunty replied, "waw, we will skin it, cook some for ourselves, dry some for later, and sell the rest". The husband replied, "no, you will cook all of it, and we will eat all of it". My aunty replied, "husband, we need to dry some and keep for later, sell some and eat some". The husband thundered, "no, we will eat all". My aunty replied, "let us cook some, dry some and eat some". The husband shouted, "what, you are disobeying me? You are disobeying me?" And he gave her some very ugly slaps, very ugly slaps".

Dulai Free Talk never married. A foolish friend told him, "You are right, Dulai Free Talk. Why would you need to have the whole cow, when you could get a pound of meat anytime you want?"

Dulai said, "Why would I come feed a total stranger for her whole life? That would be unfair to my mother, who I never had the chance to feed".

The Old Woman said to Dulai Free Talk, "your mother would have loved a daughter-in-law, at least for you to continue your father's progeny".

He replied, "I never owed my mother a daughter-in-law. If she told you that, she clearly lied. As for my father, it is better his ugliness stops with me, for no woman's beauty can dilute my ugliness in the kids I may get with her. Ugliness is strong. Was my mother not beautiful? But look what she gave birth to, ugly me, just like my father. I am as ugly as a baboon sucking lime. It is good that I'm not a woman, else this ugliness would have been more pronounced. What if I should get a daughter with this ugliness in me. Lordamasi. God forbid. Let the ugliness stop with me, let it stop with me".

"True say talk me, so let me say the truth," said The Sage. "Beauty is harder work than ugliness, it is easier to be ugly than to be beautiful. If you do nothing about yourself, ugliness sets in. Ugliness seems to be what we all move towards - sagging bodies, toothless mouths, wrinkled throats, death and its rottenness. Anyway, ugliness is in the eyes of the beholder ".

Dulai Free Talk tried his hands at various jobs. But his back talk fast-mouth got him out of these jobs very fast. A senior official told him when he worked at the quay as a security officer, "this is a different place; we don't do things like you do them up there. Here, you don't say "thief, thief" when you see someone taking some body's goods. If you really care about him not stealing, you say, "put it down, put it down". He replied, "that means you telling me this, you are also a thief".

The other time he worked as an aide to a big man in a big-big NGO. They were given DSA to go up country. The big man in the big-big NGO only gave him a quarter of DSA that was due him, and asked him to sign for the full amount. Dulai told the big man in the big-big NGO, "you've passed the mark, your corruption has no boundary: you sell seeds that must be given to poor farmers; you inflate lists of beneficiaries; you have *hide-hide* women in every project area and you corrupt the inclusion of women by only endorsing your *hide-hide* women as women's representatives in the village development committees; you've truly passed the mark, now you want me to sign for that which you did not give me; something will happen here today if you don't give me all my money".

When he worked as a foreman in a road construction company, he told an old man who accused him of sleeping with one of his wives, "I never knew Sallay was your wife. Were you not the one I mostly asked about her whereabouts when I visited her house? Were all those young women in that house your wives? Was that why you married them, to push them towards us and live off your claims of woman damage?" When the company big-men wanted to settle lots of woman-damages by withholding a small percentage of the wages of the young men in the company, Dulai Free Talk led a protest, "This is nonsense, we don't want this collusion between the companies and old chiefs to deprive us of our rights". And a word he learned during his one term at the university came up, "this is neo-feudalism; women are no meat to bait young men with".

The very first day he worked as a clearing agent, he spoke the truth about the goods he was clearing. But the government official looked at him and said, "look my friend, those goods cost more than you put in the declaration, don't lie. I will help you, give me this amount and pay that to the cashier. I'm only doing this for you". Dulai Free Talk told the official there and then, "liar, you are not doing this for me, you are doing it for yourself. You want me to feel small, like some criminal, and like you are having mercy on me, when in fact you are eating me up".

The other time, Dulai Free Talk went with Orman to buy some clothes at the Butu And Pick Market for the wedding between Santigie Ginger Da Fitter and The Beautiful Young Woman. The trader said, "it is only for you, give me this reduced amount". Dulai laughed, "do you know me, foolish man, do you know my father, do you know my mother, do you know where I stay?"

Orman told him, "the trader was only trying to make you feel special".

Dulai Free Talk replied, "so he should tell me all that story to make me feel special? No, I was not special to him; he was trying to turn me into a fool carried away by some special feeling".

At the wedding between Santigie Ginger Da Fitter and The Beautiful Young Woman, Dulai Free Talk said, "waw money has missed its way, a beautiful young woman getting married to stupid poor man. Boys, enjoy your day, it's God that pushes flies off the backside of a cow without tail".

At the wedding reception Dulai Free Talk gave the response to the toast on behalf of the guests. He entered the hall just as his name was called. He said, "Lots of activity today; and I was trying to be Bra Spider. I attended the *put kola* at the home of Pa Foday Sorry Voice, then the Mosque wedding, then waited for the *ashobi* dance round the community and for the couple to drink water at the house of the *yawo-mammy* and *okoh-daddy*, and then this reception, and then there will be a party at the house of The Young and Beautiful woman. This is too much o. This is the first time we are having this type of wedding in our community; we are not used to this. Look at this hall; this is the first time we are having a reception in a hall for a wedding in our community. And imagine, the first person to have this honour is Santigie Ginger Da Fitter. To be handsome is good; you may be lucky with beautiful women. But look at me, I'm so ugly that I saw a baboon pointing at me when the big man said, "let the ugly one go bring water". You know me now; my mouth is free. I asked The Beautiful Young Woman, "why do you want to marry Santigie Ginger?" She replied, "My mother advised me to marry a handsome ginger man who is also stupid. On telling my father he asked me to check out Momoh Ginger, and I found him to be most fitting". Okay, that may not be exactly the way she said it. You know stories change from mouth to mouth. But, say it go, say it come, stupidity could be very useful, may the protection of God cover the fools".

When Madu The Mason told him he should not have said what he said at the reception, he replied, "Foday Voice asked me to speak because he knows my mouth is as fast as foo-foo and okra down the throat; he knows my mouth is as free as the knickers of a pregnant woman; and, rain come, shine come, I will speak the truth. But you, you are a great liar. You will one day build a house of lies with your false stories; you are giving story telling a bad name".

When Santigie Ginger disappeared exactly forty months after the wedding, Dulai Free Talk said, "my fears are being confirmed, perhaps they killed him like they killed my father".

"Why would you say that," Orman The Artist asked.

"Santigie Ginger is almost an albino. I don't believe they disappear, I don't believe in all these stupid stories around".

"You and this your free talk," Orman said, "you are no longer a child, be careful about what you rub your mouth on, else you may one day rub it on cayenne pepper".

Dulai Free Talk once rubbed his mouth on the councilor, the one that Man Plus defeated. He called him Councilor Tape Rule, because that councilor would always be seen with tape rule to measure municipal lands he was busy selling. The councilor sent his boys to beat him up. Dulai Free Talk told the thugs, "if you don't beat me, I'll talk, if you beat me I'll talk more. That was how I was born".

"It is so true," said The Old Woman, "whenever Dulai's mother beat him, he would talk all he heard from his mother from the time of the last beating to the present one. I remember his mother once spanked him for being quick to take pieces of meat when he was eating with his elders. He talked

124

nonstop the whole evening. "mama told her friend that she was only eating the money of The Headmaster for nothing, her heart was still with my dead father". "Mama said Aunty Beatrice hardly washed, rather she sprayed perfumes weeks on end rather than take a bath". His mother flogged him to stop. But the more she flogged the more he talked. She stopped and begged him, "please stop, I will never flog you again"".

When the *toomboo* disease attacked the community, and the councilor came in with the government announcement that no body should touch or bury a corpse without getting papers from the authorities, Dulai Free Talk shouted, "waw, the dead now need visas to go to the land of the land".

When the councilor announced that until the government declared an end to the War Against The *Toomboo,* no body should wash corpses, Dulai Free Talk said to Momoh The Corpse Washer, "don't worry, washing is washing, transfer the skills you have learned washing corpses to washing plates for your wife's Cookery Shop, you know those two plate washers are really very slow".

Kama Bluffer died during the *War Against Toomboo*; Momoh The Corpse Washer died a few weeks after. Mamatu Cookery said to Dulai Free Talk. "My husband told me he met vomits all over

Kam Bluffer, and that his family begged him to *soutoura* his body before the Government people would come and take him away. Now my husband has died the same way Kama Bluffer died. I'm so afraid I may die like him".

"Your husband was a foolish man, I told him to concentrate on washing plates during this time, he would not listen. Now look, his shroud was not new, he was buried in the old clothes he died on. Imagine, waking up with those filthy clothes before the lord. Just imagine, just imagine".

Dulai Free Talk once told Kadia, The *Ball-eye* of Kama Bluffer, "your feet are rude; you need to give them some home training".

Kadia cussed him, "it is your mother that has rude feet".

Dulai Free Talk replied, "more".

"You are a useless man".

Dulai Free Talk replied, "more".

"You will always stand behind your fellow men".

"More".

Kadia went on cussing for over an hour, but Dulai Free Talk's only reply was, "more".

Kadia burst out crying, "you must cuss me in return; you must cuss me in return".

Dulai Free Talk replied, "more".

126

At the funeral of Kama Bluffer, The Old Imam gave this oft-repeated words at our burials, "let all those who owe Kama Bluffer own up, you may come now or later settle it with his family; likewise if he owed you something".

Ami Silencer came forward, placed on the table the most beautiful women's clothes ever seen in our community, and left without saying a word.

Dulai Free Talk said, "lordamasi, Kama Bluffer will surely need these clothes to give to the women he will be wooing in the land of the dead".

The Poda Poda Driver pushed forward to the center of the crowd where the table was. "No, no, no," he said. "Those clothes are not the property of Kama Buffer. I paid for them. Where do you think he got all the beautiful fabric he used to sew clothes for women. I brought them to him from my travels all over the country with my poda poda. I had a deal with him - he would sew for my Ami to make her happy; I would bring in the fabrics to get him to sew the most beautiful women clothes in the land. In fact he still owed me some more clothes on account of the fabrics I brought him last month and the month before".

The widows of Kama Bluffer rushed forward, fighting over the clothes, "no, no, no, you are lying, you are lying; this whole story is a lie".

In their fighting they tore some of the clothes. The Poda Poda Driver cried, "what, what, you tore the clothes, you tore the clothes?" He ran into his room, came out with a gun and shot into the air".

The mourners pushed away, except Dulai Free Talk. He walked up to The Poda Poda Driver, "The way you hold the gun reminds me of how rebels held their guns during the war. Were you a rebel or just pretending to be one?"

"I will shoot you o, I will shoot o".

Dulai Free Talk asked The Poda Poda Driver, "Will you eat me when you kill me, like they say some people did during the war? My friend, put down your gun and lets go bury Kama Bluffer before he rots in our hands".

Ami Silencer
and
The Poda Poda Driver

Shekuna, The Poda Poda Driver came to our community as a full-fledged poda poda driver; not like those other poda poda drivers who would first take months and months as apprentice poda poda drivers sleeping inside poda poda at lorry parks at night and waking up very early in the morning to wash the poda poda; after-which they would be promoted to taking months and months standing on poda poda doors to collect fares along community junctions of the land – Portee Old Road, Barracks, Low Cost Junction, Low Cost Market, Samuels, Shell, Taylor Street, Sarolla, Alpha Morlai, Kola Tik, S Bah, Banga Store, PWD, Ferry Junction, Bomeh, Akram, Up Gun Turn Table, Up Gun Market, Dan Street, Savage Square, Easton Street, Patton Street, Bombay Street, Magazine/Mountain Cut, Eastern Police and beyond; after-which these apprentice poda poda drivers would take months and months going on small errands for poda poda drivers before they would be allowed to sit behind the wheels and shown how to put on the head lights; after-which additional months and months before they would be

129

shown how to turn the ignition keys; then more months and months before they would be shown what were the clutch pedal, the accelerator pedal, the foot brake and the hand brake; after-which it would take some more months and months before they would be shown how to engage the number one, two, three and reverse gears; after-which, months more before they would be taught how to drive in the people-packed traffic of our communities; and how to be rude when they sensed they were being wronged by other drivers, especially so where the other drivers were driving private vehicles; and how to beg and beg when they hit other vehicles; and how to make cover up stories about why they had no driver's licenses on them; or stories about why they had less master-money to give to the owners of the poda poda. No, Shekuna The Poda Poda Driver did not learn about all these things whilst living in our community; he came as a full-fledged poda poda driver. He said to Dulai Free Talk on their return from burying Kama Bluffer, "this is not like before the war, when you took a long time and suffer a lot to become a poda poda driver. No, I did not take long to learn these things; I planned it, to become a poda poda driver without going through all that nonsense".

"This is lie-lie talk," said Dulai Free Talk. "Did you plan to be in a war when you were born? Did you plan to go through disarmament? Did you plan to sell the tools you told me you sold after being trained as a mechanic during the reintegration programme because people believed ex-combatants were shoddily trained and no car owner worth their salt would take their cars to them for repairs? Did you plan to meet the woman who first hired you as a driver because you toted her in heavy rains to prevent her feet getting wet in the flooded street where she had packed her vehicle to go buy some stuff at the shop where you stood outside to help people carry their things to their cars or wherever? Did you plan for the woman coming again to the shop and every time you were her favourite helper until she one day asked you if you would like to be her driver and you replied that you knew how to drive but did not have a license because the promise to get driver's licenses for ex-combatants was not fulfilled by some re-integration people? Did you plan to get this woman to get you a license to start driving her private car, until hard times fell on her and she decided to transform her private vehicle into a taxi, and she asked you to bring her money for five days a week with the sixth day being for you to get the money you must pay yourself with and the seventh day for you and the car to rest? Was that not the way you told me you started out as a taxi driver? Did you know that Ami Silencer had been keeping money from since the war and was also saving monies you gave her until one day you yourself told me that you told her that your madam was travelling and she was selling her taxi and Ami asked how much and when you told her, she got out the money and gave it to you and you bought the Taxi? Did you plan on doing away with that taxi to get some poda poda that a poda poda owner who hired your taxi grumbled about and said he would exchange his poda poda for a car plus a small amount on top because he was tired of the small master-money his poda poda driver was giving him and particularly sick of the too many stories about why that was so? Did you plan on exchanging your taxi for the man's poda poda and adding on to it monies you had been collecting which the man used to transform the taxi into a private vehicle with change to do other things? Did you plan on moving here on the insistence of Ami Silencer that you got out of the community where you had been known as a shop porter and taxi driver to this place where no one knew your previous story to start life anew as a poda poda driver? Look man, don't tell me that big-fool bellyful talk that you planned it. How many things in this place are planned? If the arrival of children here are not planned, what else about our lives can be planned?"

"True say talk me" said The Sage, "Life is mostly planned backwards; it is mostly when you are talking about life that you put a plan to it; you look at your life, and you say, oh that was the plan of my life; that was why I did well at school; that was why I fell in love with that woman; that was why God got me to be a tenant in that the house in that community."

The Poda Poda Driver said to Dulai Free Talk, 'I did not tell you about how I became a poda poda driver for you to use it against me."

"So The Poda Poda Driver was an ex-combatant," said the Teacher-writer.

"The foolish truth and reconciliation people say we must call them new citizen," said Dulai Free Talk. "They've been born again, free from their sins of war. Didn't you see the ceremonies in the junctions of the land?"

"True say talk me," said The Sage, "Many people did not want the recounting of stories of shame in the open spaces of all the generations; fathers and mothers would hide in shame at the story that they had no chance to edit for the other generations; so all that talk of forced incest and forced breastfeeding of the beheaded head of one's son and all that; all these stories blasted to the full hearing of all at the same time, that was a shameful way to tell stories. But that is the way of the times, too many stories heard by too many people at the same time, that is the source of so much disrespect now, but we must learn to live with it".

"I don't like this talk about the war; it is bad," said The Poda Poda Driver, as he walked away.

But not long after that, about three hours, forty three minutes and fifty seconds he came running back to the junction, like some hen being chased by a cock. Look, I was there, I timed him myself, I am not like those other story tellers who make up stories about this and this. You just ask people in our community, The Poda Poda Driver came running back to the junction and said "I need people to help me beg her, she's leaving me. She said I did not hide my story well, that everybody now knows that I was amongst the bad men of the war."

"And so?" Dulai Free Talk asked. "Is your evil more than the evil of those we no longer care about? Do our people not say however much a son has defecated, his father would have defecated more than him; you are a son of the war, the fathers of the war defecated much more. Or are you of a new breed of sons who would defecate more than their fathers ever did?"

"This is no laughing matter," said The Poda Poda Driver. "I'm serious, I'm serious, where is The Ladani? I want him to go help me beg her".

"Seriousness is in the Labour Ward," Dulai Free Talk replied, "but even there, they laugh at the way some women cry —"Amadu, where are you? The two of us enjoyed it, now I'm the only one in pain" or "my waist bone is on fire, please bring the fire brigade," or "mama, mama, you never told me it would be so, mama, mama you lied o, you lied o mama." Seriousness is at the graveyard, but even there, we talk-talk idle talks 'bout man-and-woman business sitting on the gravestones of the dead — "when are you going to your girl friend today?" or "if you were to choose between a big breasted woman and big-waist woman, whom would you choose?" or "father-in-law or mother-in-law, if you were to choose the one to die first, who would you want dead?" Seriousness was the war; but even about it, we tell many funny stories about behaviour of people when they beheld the horrors of those days. So my friend, don't threaten us with seriousness. Let us just go with The Ladani to Ami Silencer".

The begging mission led by The Ladani met Councilor Man Plus with Ami Silencer; she was telling Ami Silencer, "he must leave, not you. You have spent more time inside this house than Shekuna. The time for women to leave is passed; now it is the men that must leave the house".

The Ladani said to Councilor Man Plus, "what, instead of putting out the fire you are adding petrol unto it?"

Councilor Man Plus replied, "this is not a prayer thing; this is a state thing; a man can no longer force a woman out".

"I'm not forcing her out," said The Poda Poda Driver, "she's the one who does not want to stay".

"What's the true story here?" asked the Ladani

"We are having lots and lots of stories here. What's the true story here?" asked Councilor Man Plus

"True say talk me," said The Sage, "there's no true story, all are made up. The story that is better made up is what we call the true story".

"I will tell you our story," said Ami Silencer

The news spread around, people gathered; the community was hungry for Ami Silencer's side of the story.

It was getting to night, the place was little dark. A circle formed around Ami Silencer. She placed a

136

bench on the part of the circle that had fewer people, and she began, like storytellers long ago began their stories, "in," she said

"Out," the junction-crowd roared".

"I was a college student when men with arms struck our dormitories in the darkness of an early morning that I would never forget. A gang of them took four of us away with them. I was twenty then. Shekuna was the leader of the gang who took us. He said he wanted the most beautiful woman amongst the abductees, and they brought us to him at sunrise. We stood in line, the four of us – Nakama, Yeama, me and Mballu. I was the third person in the line. He checked the first two, holding their chins up to properly see their faces, and squeezing their breasts and buttocks. My turn came. But the soonest our eyes met, he started crying.

"Why?" his men asked him.

"She looks like my twin-sister, exactly the same as she was when we lost track of each other as we ran away when our village was attacked.".

One of the men said, "well then she's your sister."

"She could not be her, even if you write the letter 'A' as big as a cotton tree, my sister would not understand, for she never went to school, and this woman here is a college student. I lost track of my twin-sister seven years ago, so even though she looked like this woman when I lost her, she would be much older than this woman now."

Bravery took over me, and I told him, "I may be your sister; you never know the ways of our fathers. Was your father a road construction worker?"

It was a question that just came into my head. Perhaps it was because stories of road construction workers were ingrained in me. Perhaps it was because I was thinking too much of what my mother told me about road construction fathers who abandoned their children. Perhaps it was because I felt abandoned that I asked that question. Whatever it was, it changed everything.

"Yes, yes," Shekuna replied. "my mother told me my father was a foreman with a road construction company; but that he vanished with the road, leaving my mother pregnant with us."

"Me too, my mother told me my father was a road construction worker. I never knew him. He vanished with the road; running away from an old man that my mother was betrothed to. They called me a child of the road. Perhaps the same man was responsible for our birth. I could be your sister, your younger sister of the same father".

That endeared me to Shekuna, the possibility that we are of the same father. And that also saved the friends that were with me. Shekuna became our protector. Four beautiful women around him; four beautiful women that he should protect from the badness of the war. But we lost all of them, save me.

Some of his men thought that Nakama, Yeama, Mballu and I were softening him, making him lose his appetite for war and rape and pillage. They didn't like that, and they decided to put a stop to it by killing the three other women. I believed they left me out because they thought killing a sister of the commander might give them a story that would be very hard to cover up. Nakama was killed first, waylaid on some forest path and hacked to death. We found her body parts all over the paths. Some people said somebody might have killed her for ritual purposes —her tongue removed to give the murderer eloquence and commanding voice over others; her palms removed to give the killer money, that everything he touched turned to wealth; her private parts removed, to give her killer great potency in what ever he did; her soles flayed, to give her killer a gait of command, a presence of great standing; and the skin of her thighs and back skinned, to sew for the killer a cloth of human skin, extra-protection against the bad-hearts and bad-darts of others. But I didn't believe the ritual murder story; something inside my heart told me that was not the case. Yeama was the second to die; they told us she was shot as she tried to escape with the stories of our movements to the enemy. We doubted the story, but what they told us fit in nicely with the prevailing evil and fear, so that story won the day. Third to die was Mballu. We found her corpse in an abandoned diamond pit seven days after she disappeared from our side of the camp; all her body was buried in the mud, save for her right hand, with her index

139

figure pointing up to the sky, as if she was calling on the heavens to witness was had befallen her. Story-tellers of her death reminded us that she had eyes for diamonds, and had on occasions spotted diamonds sparkling in the muds of the night; and that she might have gone over at night to the pits to look for the stones, and had paid the ultimate price, because some stones, being devils did not like persons with such searing eyes as Mballu. All sorts of stories came out that day.

But the real stories about the deaths of Nakama, Yeama and Mballu did not stay hidden for long. I found out who killed them and I cried to Shekuna for revenge. Shekuna wanted revenge, because he had seen Nakama, Yeama, and Mballu as his own family in the bush. So he shot the guys who murdered them. Pandemonium broke out. News leaked to the high command about what happened. They sent people to take Shekuna to their council of justice. He knew it meant death; I knew it meant death. We had never heard of anybody standing trial before that council and not being condemned to die for this or that anti-revolutionary crimes. Shekuna escaped with me; we came to this town and joined the disarmament process. But eking out a living was tough until he came by a woman who hired him as a taxi driver".

The Ladani asked, "so you are a daughter of war?"

Ami Silencer replied, "I don't like that story of me".

"Well then," Dulai Free Talk said, "you are child of the road."

"Though it saved me once," Ami Silencer replied, "I also don't like that story of me. I am ashamed of it; to be a child of an unknown father".

"Where were you born?" Dulai Free Talk asked.

Ami Silencer told him.

"Who was your mother?"

Ami Silencer replied, "Sallay".

Dulai Free Talk burst out laughing, "lordamasi, lordamasi, no wonder, no wonder."

"What is it, what is it?" Ami Silencer asked

"She was a most beautiful woman, Sallay, with a big black pretty mark on the underneath of her left breast. I called it her God-mark, the mark by which God marked her for me. But I left that village not because of that old man asking for woman damage. I left because I thought any child born to me would be as ugly as I. I was running away from the possibility of another ugly being like me. But look at you, so beautiful. Look at you, look at you". He hugged Ami Silencer, as a father would hug his daughter.

The Old Imam said, "what a story!"

The Ladani said, "what a story!"

The Old Woman said, "your blood is your blood".

The community shouted, "blood is blood".

Dulai Free Talk turned to Shekuna, The Tax Driver, "where were you born?"

He told him.

"No, I never worked on road construction along that route, never. You are not my son, she's not your sister; the book on resemblances say because we are not very different from each other, we sometimes meet people who may look very much like people we know. She is not your sister".

"I thank God, I thank God, that was the only thing holding us back. I love Ami more than anything else in this world".

Dulai Free Talk said to the crying Ami, "please forgive him. Please forgive us".